# Last Train To Noir City

**Underground Voices**
http://www.undergroundvoices.com
**Edited by Cetywa Powell**
**2010**

www.undergroundvoices.com

Printed in the United States of America

ISBN-978-0-9830456-0-1

# TABLE OF CONTENTS

# THE FACE

## Sean C. Hayden

Leonard Moody blinked, leaned forward, squinted, backed up, and blinked again. The face was still there. Leonard, dressed only in what he called his bathrobe, but was actually a hospital gown he'd filched from Townsville Medical Center during his last admission, stared dumbfounded into his toilet bowl. An unlit Camel cigarette hung from the corner of his mouth.

"Fuck," he muttered, "I just shit a Jesus face."

Instinctively, Leonard reached for the flush handle, but his hand froze on the lever. This, Leonard thought, must be worth something to someone. After all, he reasoned, people were finding Jesus faces in all kinds of things: potatoes, pieces of toast, water stains, frosted windows, egg salad sandwiches, but this was the first time, as far as he knew, that Jesus had appeared in a piece of shit.

Leonard sprinted from the bathroom, stubbed his toe in the living room, and picked up the telephone in the kitchen.

"Fuck," he shouted, hopping on one foot, dialing, and trying to light his cigarette all at the same time.

"Four One One information," a woman's voice said.

"Yah, gimmie the newspaper," Leonard panted, breathless.

"Which newspaper are you looking for sir?"

"Any newspaper. I don't know. The big one."

\* \* \* \*

Leonard, no longer in his hospital robe, but dressed in his finest bicycle shorts and Mr. Doughnut tee shirt, stood beside and slightly behind the reporter from The Blabber Mouth, Townsville's largest newspaper.

"See?" He said, pointing over the reporter's shoulder, "See? There's a face. Do you see the face?"

"I do see a face," the reporter said, "but it doesn't look like Jesus. It looks like John Lennon."

"What are you talking about?"

"Yah," the reporter said, "It looks exactly like John Lennon. Don't you see the glasses?"

Leonard did, in fact, see the glasses, but it never occurred to him that Jesus of Nazareth hadn't worn glasses.

"This is amazing," the reporter went on, "Sammy, get in here and take some pictures of this."

Sammy, the photographer, was standing in the hallway smoking a cigarette and wondering why he didn't work for Better Homes and Gardens, or National Geographic, or Hustler. He slouched into the bathroom muttering something about wasted talent when he looked into the toilet bowl and froze.

"Jesus fucking Christ," Sammy whispered.

"No, it's John Lennon," Leonard corrected.

* * * *

When the story broke, people came from everywhere. At first, Leonard just let them in. They jostled about the toilet bowl snapping pictures and shoving each other for a better look. They stood on their tiptoes and peered over each other's shoulders. They said things like "That's amazing," and "I've never seen anything like it," and "Congratulations. You must be so proud."

Leonard enjoyed the attention, but attention wasn't what he sought. What he sought, was money. He began charging admission. Five dollars a head. It wasn't much, but with more than a hundred visitors per day, it added up. Eventually, he had a velvet rope installed around the toilet bowl. Thank God, Leonard through, I have a second bathroom.

Leonard spent his days collecting money, smiling, and answering questions.

"I was just sitting there reading TV Guide...

"It didn't feel like anything special when it was coming out, but when I stood up, there it was...

"No, I don't even like The Beatles. I'm an Elvis fan...

"What do I think it means? Well, I guess it means that we should love one another...

People generally cheered when he said that.

* * * *

One afternoon, as Leonard was fielding Beatles questions and signing autographs, a fat shrill-voiced woman collapsed in a heap beside the toilet bowl. "Oh my God!" The woman screamed, "John Lennon's gone!"

Leonard's heart sank. He had feared this. How long, after all, could a piece of shit last before it disintegrated? But when he pushed his way into the bathroom, ready to flush the bowl once and for all, a new face stared up at him from the water. Leonard squinted his eyes. Now the shit looked exactly like Fidel Castro.

"I can't believe this," someone shouted. "Fidel Castro! What a rip off!"

"Listen everyone," Leonard said facing the crowd, "I'm as confused as you are. I don't know what happened."

"Five dollars for Fidel Castro!" Someone shouted from the back of the apartment, "I'm getting out of here."

One by one the Beatles fans filed out. They shook their heads and muttered to themselves. Leonard distinctly heard someone use the word, "scam."

Scam? They had been privy to a magic shit. How could they be disappointed?

\* \* \* \*

It was all over Townsville. The John Lennon shit had morphed into Fidel Castro. For days, no one came. Leonard realized that John Lennon was far more popular than Castro, but still, a magic shit was a magic shit. He thought more people would have been interested. Leonard pondered the inexplicable nature of human curiosity while purchasing a pack of smokes from his local grocer.

"Good morning Leonard," the store's proprietor said with his usual inscrutable expression, "I save last pack of unfilter Camel for you."

"Thank you, Mr. Quan."

"You know Leonard, you do very bad thing when you make Castro shit. Castro very bad man. You should make another shit, only this time, make George Harrison."

"I'll try Mr. Quan."

"Rile my guitaaaar, gentry reeps," Mr. Quan sang.

Leonard stepped out of Mr. Quan's grocery and blinked in the morning sunlight. He started the two and a half block trek to his apartment building. Already wheezing after half a block, he stopped, opened his freshly purchased package of unfiltered Camel cigarettes, tapped the bottom of the pack with his forefinger and popped one in his mouth.

"There he is," someone shouted, "The Castro lover."

Leonard looked up dumbly. A group of visibly incensed men and women stood clustered on the opposite side of the street. One of the men sported a tee shirt with the words, FREEDOM ISN'T FREE spelled out across the chest in big black letters.

Castro lover? Thought Leonard.

"That guy hates America!" someone else shouted.

A fat angry woman twisted her face into an ugly scowl and hurled her bottle of diet peach Snapple across the street. The bottle shattered on the pavement a few feet away from where Leonard stood. Bewildered, Leonard remained rooted, too shocked to move. When a second bottle shattered on the ground beside him, this one much closer than the first, he turned and ran. Cries of "pinko," "commie," and "terrorist," echoed behind him.

Leonard ran two blocks in the wrong direction and stopped short. Suddenly seized in a grip he was all too familiar with, he clutched his chest. Sweat soaked and panting, Leonard fumbled in his pockets for his nitroglycerine, found the bottle, and popped one of the small white tablets under his tongue. Within minutes, the crushing pain dissipated.

Six years earlier, when Leonard suffered the first of four heart attacks, he'd told the emergency room doctor that it felt like an elephant was sitting on his chest. Since then, whenever Leonard feels the onset of angina pectoris, he imagines an elephant, a great shaggy Snufalufagus only he can see, a rank, obese, cigarette smoking elephant, straddling him and sitting on his chest.

When his wheezing subsided, Leonard wiped the sweat from his forehead and lit a cigarette. Ten minutes later, he was standing outside of his apartment building. Someone had spray painted the words, "COMMIE GO HOME!" on the front door.

Go home? He was home. He'd lived there for fifteen years.

\* \* \* \*

Leonard was at a loss. Nobody wanted to see the Castro shit. Beyond that, it had become a liability. People sent him hate mail, shouted insults at him, defaced his property and occasionally, threw bottles at him. He had finally made up his mind to flush the toilet when the doorbell rang. Cautiously, Leonard pressed the intercom talk button.

"It's late," Leonard said, "what do you want?"

"Mr. Moody," a young female voice sounded over the intercom, "it's an honor to speak with you."

"Who are you?" Leonard said.

"We are members of the Townsville University Revolutionary Division. We are here to see the likeness of Comrade Fidel."

"You're not going to throw bottles at me?" Leonard asked.

"Bottles? Most certainly not."

The Townsville University Revolutionary Division consisted of four Townsville University students, two boys and two girls, dressed in matching black berets and turtlenecks. After they had seen the Castro shit and commented on its stunning accuracy and congratulated Leonard for his accomplishment, the group's leader, Comrade Gerald, a tall cow eyed young man, called a formal meeting in Leonard's apartment. Leonard was named as guest of honor.

They arranged themselves in a circle in the living room. A young woman with black horn rim glasses, short hair, and an even shorter skirt, sat beside Leonard on the sofa. She introduced herself as Comrade Ava, and offered Leonard her hand. Leonard shook Ava's small soft hand and blushed brightly.

As Comrade Gerald read out the bullets for discussion, he was interrupted by the sound of slurping. All eyes turned to a heavyset youth busily sucking a large soda through a plastic straw.

"Is that soft drink from McDonald's, Comrade Dwayne?" Gerald asked.

Comrade Dwayne squirmed in his seat. "What? I was hungry," he said sheepishly, "I stopped on the way here."

"Don't you know that McDonald's is a corporate fascist entity breaking the backs of the proletariat?"

"Well," Comrade Dwayne said after a moment's hesitation, "you packed your lunch in plastic Tupperware. Plastic! Do you have any idea what that does to your Carbon Footprint?"

"At least I'm a vegetarian!" Comrade Gerald said.

Dwayne's fleshy face went red, and his bottom lip quivered. Without another word, he stood up and ran out of the apartment.

"Oh Gerald," said a slender young woman with long black hair, "You can be such an ass."

"It's not my fault if comrade Dwayne can't handle the truth. I'm sick and tired of being the moral conscience of this movement."

"Moral conscience? You're so glib."

"Glib? My therapist says that I'm a very creative person!" Gerald shouted and stormed out of the apartment. The slender woman ran out after him trumpeting apologies, leaving Leonard alone with Ava.

"Sorry about your meeting" Leonard managed.

"That always happens," Ava said. "In fact, that was one of our longest meetings."

"Oh."

"But you're not like the others," Ava said, taking Leonard's hand and sliding it under her skirt, "You're a true revolutionary."

Leonard was not sure how moving his bowels had made him a revolutionary, but he didn't argue.

\* \* \* \*

When Leonard woke the next morning, Ava was glaring at him from across the room.

"You pretended to be a revolutionary just so you could sleep with me," she said.

"What?"

"I suppose you think I'm a sinner. I guess you think I'm going to hell! Well you can save the sanctimony."

"Huh?"

"Oh don't try to bullshit me. I went into the bathroom this morning while you were sleeping and I saw it."

"What?"

"You bible thumpers are all the same. Perverts and cheats."

Ava stormed out of the bedroom. Leonard heard the door slam shut when she left the apartment.

Well that was strange, Leonard thought, but then, women had always puzzled him. Rubbing the crust from his eyes, he sat up, fumbled for a cigarette and shuffled to the bathroom.

"Holy Shit," Leonard said aloud. His cigarette dropped from his mouth and landed on his bare foot. Leonard jumped up, hopped backwards on one leg, and fell on his ass. This time there was no mistaking it. Beard, humble upturned eyes, crown of thorns; the picture a study of suffering and grace, Jesus Christ bobbed serenely in the bowl.

Leonard got up, shook his head, limped to the kitchen, and prepared his usual breakfast: Atenolol 200mg, Lisinopril 40mg, Lasix 80mg, Aspirin 325mg, one multivitamin, two cups of black coffee, and an unfiltered Camel cigarette. After breakfast, he picked up the telephone and called The Blabbermouth.

* * * *

Predictably, the Jesus shit made a bigger splash than the John Lennon shit and the Castro shit combined. People came from miles around to gaze upon the likeness of the Son of God. The sick, the blind, the crippled, the insane, all came to Townsville.

Before long, Townsville, never a popular tourist destination, was overrun. The hotels were booked solid for weeks in advance. The streets were choked with traffic, and on any given day, people lined up for blocks outside Leonard's apartment building.

At first, the Townsville Police tried to disperse the crowds, but when The Blabbermouth ran a few front-page photographs of police officers strong-arming cripples who'd traveled for days hoping for a miracle cure, public opinion swayed city officials towards a different approach.

Leonard's street was cordoned off from traffic, bottled water was distributed free of charge, and a string of Porta-Potties were deposited.

Pilgrim's Village was born.

At first, Leonard was pleased. Once again, his shit was the talk of the town and the money was rolling in; but he soon grew weary. The street outside his apartment building had been transformed into a three-ring circus. Leonard was afraid to go outside. The media were always waiting for him. He couldn't even go to the corner to buy a pack of cigarettes from Mr. Quan without being accosted by pilgrims and the paparazzi.

Finally, Leonard barred his door to the public all together, but it didn't slow the influx of people. Day after day, more pilgrims arrived in Townsville and camped outside Leonard's apartment building. In a few short weeks, Pilgrim's Village had grown into a teeming shantytown, and Leonard had become a prisoner in his own home.

* * * *

Prior to the magic shit, Leonard's only source of income had been his monthly disability check, but prior to his disability —a herniated disk sustained during some truly inspired hip gyration—

Leonard had been a relatively successful Elvis impersonator. Although he still possessed a superb singing voice, Leonard found himself utterly unable to channel The King as he once had. The emotional pain was too great.

Fed up with his sequestered existence, Leonard opened his bedroom closet and dug out his old Elvis costume. He'd gained a little weight since he'd stopped working but felt certain he could still squeeze into it, post-traumatic stress be dammed.

Resplendent in a white sequined jumpsuit, black pompadour wig, stick on mutton chop sideburns, and extra large orange sunglasses, Leonard Moody, through his bedroom window, breeched the cool night and descended, with great effort, the fire-escape.

Once safely on the pavement, Leonard slipped up the alleyway and emerged through the shadows onto the main street. Disguised as he was, Leonard was able to walk with complete anonymity through the crowds who had taken up residence in front of his apartment building.

Under most circumstances, a man so fat he stretched an Elvis suit to its limit would stand out in a crowd, but in Pilgrim's Village, Leonard hardly managed to engender a raised eyebrow. There, amidst the all night cook fires burning in garbage cans, the bible waving bag ladies speaking in tongues, the stench of unwashed bodies and overflowing Porta-Potties, the wailing throngs of lost souls seeking divine recognition, the psalm singing and the gnashing of teeth, the groups of men and women with arms upraised to the Lord and toilet seats around their necks, Leonard moved unrecognized.

Once past the police barricades, Leonard headed towards the park. Seeking solitude, he traced his way through crisscrossing side streets, avoiding the main thoroughfares. As the Carnival din of Pilgrim's Village dissipated, Leonard's mood lightened.

What to do now? That was the question. Certainly, Leonard was pleased that his shit had morphed into a less contentious figure. No one, after all, would throw bottles at the guy who had shit Jesus. But being the custodian of a piece of magical excrement was fast becoming a larger burden than it was worth. He had made a great deal of money. It would be a simple matter to flush Jesus down the crapper and retire.

Leonard's silent reverie was severed by the sputtering rumble of a bulky black panel van in desperate need of a new exhaust system. Leonard looked up in time to see the van's side door slide open and discharge several masked figures wielding short stout clubs. Before the hefty Elvis impersonator could say, Thank you very much, one of the clubs came down with a thwack, and everything went black.

* * * *

Leonard woke with a hatchet-like pain in the center of his skull. He tried to roll over, but his left arm held fast. With reluctance, Leonard opened his eyes, finding himself sprawled naked on a wooden floor and handcuffed to a radiator.

"Mr. Moody," a voice said.

Through hazy waves of nauseating pain, Leonard saw an obese woman dressed in the 18th century garb of a Mormon fundamentalist.

"Are you awake, Mr. Moody?" Her voice was both fluid and nauseating, like an oil slick.

"Who are you? Where am I?" Leonard managed.

"Who I am is not important," the glaring, pie faced woman said.

Leonard tried to get up, and was reminded by the biting pain in his wrist, that he was restrained.

"Listen," Leonard said, "I've got money. Just let me go and I'll give you whatever you want."

The woman's eyes gleamed like nickels, and her pink tongue darted in and out of her mouth. "But you've already given us what we want."

"I have a medical condition," Leonard pleaded, "I need my medications. You have to let me go."

"We have seen the sign, Mr. Moody."

"Sign?"

"In your bathroom. The sign of the coming of the end of days."

Leonard looked up in time to see the woman bring a club down on his head. He felt the room tilt and the world swim, and fell, once more, into unconsciousness.

When Leonard woke next, it was to the sound of hammers. There were more people in the room this time. The fat woman from before was there, along with several cross-eyed children, all dressed as though they'd just stepped out of an Amish village. A burly man with a thick tangle of curly orange hair was on his knees swinging a claw hammer, while a short bald-headed man held a wooden beam across another. When they had finished, the two men hefted their creation.

Leonard squinted his eyes. The roughly fashioned crucifix swam in and out of focus.

"You are the risen Lord made flesh," the round faced woman with the toxic voice chirped, "you are the lamb, you are the blood sacrifice."

"Huh…? What…?" Leonard sputtered.

"In the garden of Gethsemane, Jesus questioned. It is a mystery how God can be both pawn and king, but it is a glorious mystery."

"Listen," Leonard said, suddenly awash with fear's stark clear-headed sobriety, "I'm not whatever you think I am. I'm not anybody. All I did was take a shit."

"Is it time Momma?" one of the children said, hopping from one foot to the other.

The moon-faced matriarch nodded, her eyes twinkling.

Leonard was unfastened from the radiator, pulled to his feet, and thrown down upon the cross. The two men began lashing Leonard's arms to the arms of the crucifix. They cinched the ropes tight, stretching his arms to the point of breaking. Pain blossomed brightly. His vision dimmed.

Leonard watched the moon-faced woman squat beside him and hold a nail against his open palm. The man with the shock of orange hair handed her his hammer. Leonard opened his mouth to plead, but his voice had deserted him. Over the woman's shoulder, he saw his Snufalufagus shuffling towards him.

The elephant shifted its weight from foot to foot, lolled his shaggy head, and eased itself down on Leonard's chest. Leonard, feeling the all too familiar leaden weight, thought instinctively, fleetingly, about the nitroglycerine tablets he didn't have. He felt his heart rate climb. Thirsting for oxygen, he gasped and sputtered. Pearls of icy sweat coated his skin. Soaking wet, panting, shivering, Leonard closed his eyes. He could hear the sound of hammering from far away.

The elephant yawned, stretched, and slept. Leonard Moody saw no more.

\* \* \* \*

Ava pulled the black wool ski mask from her head. Her close-cropped hair was soaked with sweat. It was far too hot for the ski mask, but she was unpracticed as a burglar. Armed with a pair of salad tongs and a plastic beach pail, she tiptoed through Leonard's apartment. Once in the bathroom, she held her breath, leaned over the rim, and peered into toilet. An entirely new visage floated idle in the bowl.

"Amazing," she gasped, "it looks just like her."

Having secured the booty, Ava slipped out through the same window she had entered. Why, she thought, should a dishonest cheat like Leonard Moody, be the guardian of such important poo? Poo like that should belong to everyone. This wasn't theft, she reasoned, it was liberation.

Her plastic pail sloshing softly by her side, Ava descended the fire escape and disappeared into the night.

# IN THE BELLY OF THE PIG

## S. Hemming

The snow never settles, and the sun is never warm enough to take the chill away.

Each breath sends tiny electric shocks through the fillings in your teeth and your fingers tingle in the frigid air. There is a threat of sleet in the sky and you know that as you stand beneath lead-coloured clouds you will inevitably have to drag weary feet through dirty sludge.

I know there are many contradictions in nature, many slight nuances in the fabric of life. Some are obvious, like sunlight and snow, while others exist in the periphery, lurking like diseased spectres on the edge of reason, in the heart of darkness.

We stand together now, my colleagues and I, blowing into cupped palms, making overlapping footprints where our boots grind into the rapidly thawing snow of the night before.

As a single unit we stare down at the spread-eagled figure lying dismembered and bloodied at our feet. There are no regrets, no false sympathy, for this person deserved all he had received. This terrible man had inflicted ungodly abuse on all those he had ever come into contact with. He had cut a swathe of misery across the whole of the midlands for ten years. He had killed annually and had foiled each and every attempt at discovery.

Until now.

And I am tired of the chase. My bones ache like those of a man twenty years older, and I have been reliably informed that the lines on my face reflect every lost lead, each snippet of misinformation, every thrust of my dogged determination into the nooks and crannies of this, my home, the belly of the pig.

I look up into eggshell blue and the perfect stillness of sepia clouds, and I wonder what might have been, had I done things differently. Would lives have been saved? Would my own life have taken a less traumatic turn?

He had always been one step ahead, always that goading arrogance; and the letters written in his victims' blood. Naming me, as he liked to call me, his prime antagonist, and always ending in a row of kisses. A pyramid of meticulously aligned crosses: but not the victims blood these, someone else's; probably, we had thought, his own. I assumed I had become immune to his loathsome taunts, but knew deep down that with each tantalising note he was infecting me with a part of himself. A worm of doubt had burrowed into my conscience and slowly, inexorably, it was eating away at the very essence of my moral fortitude, my integrity and my honour.

You see, I had wanted this man dead. No, not just dead, butchered. Torn and ragged was how I wanted him. Much as he is now.

This monster now crucified before us reminds me of ten years of fruitless, agonising, defeat. In all my thirty-two years in the job I have never experienced such a depraved soul, nor one so utterly indifferent to suffering. Nor, indeed, one so completely compelling.

Nor one I feel such an affinity with.

For it is a truth that the curse of obsession, by its very nature - and especially when dealing with something you thought was the opposite of yourself - draws you inevitably into the bleakness of fascination. As a detective you must imagine yourself to be that person. You must conjure up his own dark fantasies and, while maintaining sanity, you must anticipate his urges and pre-empt his awful deeds. I have worried more than once that I may be slipping into the same evil quagmire out of which he had crawled. I have had many sleepless nights twisted into the damp folds of my sodden quilt. Nightmares and the sickness of his degenerate acts writhe in my mind and torture that twilight moment before waking.

This man had not just killed but had defiled each of the young women he had so mercilessly stalked and targeted. His ferocity knew no bounds. Where he is now is where he should have been ten years ago.

So why then am I so devoid of emotion? Why is it my friends and colleagues cast such strange looks at me? And why the whispered comments after each furtive glance?

I look down on the figure of Terrence Blanck and see only the carcass of a rabid dog. He had long since rejected the mantle of Humanity and was now only a clouded caricature. He was a virus far-flung into the lives of ten innocent people, destroying many more in the process. I have no right to compare him to a disease which has the possibility of cure when so many young women had pleaded and begged for his mercy.

We had all seen the footage. Watched through tears of shame and impotence. Railed at his cackling laugh as he killed them one by one.

So now we look on in silence with the wind sighing through metallic brown leaves. Small flurries of sleet blow this way and that, caught in the spiral of an Autumn breeze.

And I feel nothing in my cold heart.

No joy, no relief. Just closure. The end of a quest which has estranged family and friends, ruined my marriage, and propelled my kids into the heartfelt affection of a man I had once called mate. That same man who now listens to the mellow eloquence of Blind Willie McTell singing Rollin' Mama Blues on my Wharfedales, in the comfort of my Parker Knoll while stroking the hair of a woman called Emma whom I had once called wife.

I harbour no animosity toward her, even less toward Doug, who has been a better husband in their two years of marriage than I had ever been in the twenty years previous. And I could not blame my sons for hating me, nor for beating me to a pulp when at the height of my compulsive obsession I had directed my anger and frustration toward their Mother. Only my daughter Beth, she of the sweet voice and alabaster skin, sends me the odd letter, albeit from Australia, purporting to understand my weaknesses when really she has no idea.

I had always been aware of a special bond between Doug and Emma though I am sure it had been purely platonic at that time. The fact that they became lovers only a couple of months after I moved out did not surprise me perhaps as much as it should have.

But that's okay. I am resigned to my loneliness. Glenmorangie and the likes of Big Bill Broonzy and Lightnin' Hopkins take the edge off my shame and blur my fears for the future.

In a way I was glad for them both, and, selfishly, back then, I knew that it meant I could concentrate all my efforts on finding the killer. It had become such a personal mission that even my superiors began, eventually, to question whether or not I was the right man for the job.

My perspective had been compromised - or so they said - by personal problems caused by the investigation. Of course this was true. But, as I had explained at the time, it was a disruption that could only help, rather than hinder, my single-minded search for the killer.

The tabloids, they said, were castigating me at every turn. Fuck 'em, I said. But they rule the consciousness of the masses, they argued. Maybe so, I replied, but they don't, and never will, understand the process of finding someone as insidious as the monster we sought.

And so it went on.

And the only way I remained as head of the investigation was because, after all these years, no-one else wanted it. I had the manpower and the money, unlimited resources at my disposal. Forensics drew a blank at every turn, snitches knew nothing; I combed the gun-ridden catacombs of cities like Nottingham and Birmingham; interrogated with ultra violence the dark denizens of these inhospitable places. I delved and dug and dissected every criminal procedure in every text book. I even part-mastered the intricacies of my arch-enemy: the computer.

But I found nothing.

Nothing, that is, until I sat one night in my darkened bed-sit reviewing for the umpteenth time the sickening tapes the killer has made of his barbarities. At least the first seven were tapes, on VHS format. These last two had been transferred to disc, like he was digitalising his sickness. There have been nine till now and I have watched them so many times they are a part of my everyday life. I force myself to observe every detail, as I have a thousand times before.

Twelve-year old malt slides with a peaty burn into a stomach devoid of food as the start of a throbbing migraine scratches behind my eyes.

I am two-thirds of the way through the ninth tape when there comes a knock at my door. It is the sleazy, muffled double-tap I know can only be my landlord. There is only one reason for him to call at any time other than for his rent, which I had paid the day before yesterday…

… a parcel has been delivered.

I sit cross-legged on the floor. My fingers leak sweat, stains brown wrapping, smudges the end letters of my name and address.

With trembling hands I insert the disc into the old reconditioned computer before me. I watch for half an hour, guilt and shame hand-in-hand with morbid curiosity, as he stalks and taunts his prey through a labyrinth of ply-wood walls and plasterboard corridors, a maze of his own design in a building which had to be both spacious and remote. We know this because he never ties nor gags nor restrains his victims in any way. Although there is never any sound on the tapes, their terrified fleeing and desperate scrabbling at immovable obstacles tells its own story.

Sobbing contractions throw my shoulders forward and back. My tears feel like hot wax. Greasy sweat drenches me in a lather of impotence. Acid burns my empty stomach, searching for something to digest.

As with the previous tapes, the poor, fleeing child is well aware she is being followed, not only by her tormentor, but by banks of cameras which track her every terrified move. She rebounds from wall to wall. She has a wide, agonised expression which is lifted and stretched by the grotesquery of fish-eye lenses: arms flail, hands twitch, clapping, fingers coming together, entwined, parting.

I swipe moisture from my face with the back of my hand as I lean closer to the screen. Her sweet, innocent face fills my vision but it is her hands which trap my attention.

I snatch for my mobile, drop it, frantically dial a number where it lay on the floor, the side of my face pressed into the threadbare carpet as I wait for a connection.

A friend of mine – one of the few I haven't driven away by my boorish and arrogant obsession - is a computer geek. A young man who had befriended me at a local college as I struggled to understand the complexities of the internet. He simplified the entire process for me and, though I found his intellect daunting at first, I began to nurture a grudging respect for his patience when dealing with my obvious inadequacies.

An hour later James Barclay turns up at my bed-sit. The second he steps into my room I have him by the throat. I can smell weed on his breath and in his dishevelled attire and in a plume of whisky fumes I snarl at him:

"You say nothing about what you're about to see, do you understand?"

His floppy fringe flaps and waves in front of eyes, enlarged by coke-bottle glasses. After a stuttering assurance that his lips are sealed I drag him bodily to the computer and play the part of the tape I want him to see.

"What does that look like to you?" I blurt. He turns to look at me. I cuff the back of his head. "Look at it. Her hands, man, her hands!"

"Look's like sign language," he states simply.

The words hit me with the force of a vocal tsunami. I can't catch my breath. My heart beats a rapid tattoo in my chest as a surge of adrenaline floods my system.

Even as I watch the helpless victim's frantic communication with an outside world she has no idea is there, I cannot help but admire her strength of character: her terrified countenance flicks left and right; then back, over her shoulder. A shadow passes between her and the camera, a spectral image of darkened rage, a tapered silhouette raised above her. Then her final, silent scream......

I reach over James' shoulder and press pause. For all his pretensions of being abroad in the modern world, this is one scene I have no wish for him to witness. I have seen it nine times before. I know what is about to happen. He looks up at me with an expression of knowing concern, as if he knows what it means to me.

I am across the room in an instant, rooting through piles of discarded junk until I find what I'm searching for. A quick flip through the Yellow Pages and my finger follows a line of deaf schools and associated institutions. I make a frantic phone call, insisting that I am indeed a policeman and begging for an e-mail address so I can send something which could save the lives of many more unfortunate children. Despite initial scepticism the address is given and after thanking her profusely, I ask her to stay on the line and turn to James.

"Send her the part with the hands. Nothing more."

An agonising wait ensues. Moments pass. I can hear what sounds like well-manicured fingernails drumming a light beat on cold plastic. Maybe even a slight gasp as she realises what she is seeing. The she tells me what she thinks the young girl had been signing.. It was, she said, difficult to interpret as the young girl was obviously a novice but the best she could come up with was - and here my heartbeat increased twofold as I held my breath - what she came up with was: O.N.G.I.T.C.H.

I look at James. He shrugs. My mind reels with possibilities.

"Well...?" I yell. "You're the geek! What do you think?"

James' eyebrows come together. He stares at the letters. His fingers fly over the keyboard. His eyes flicker.

"You say wherever he lives has to be remote. The countryside maybe. And we're certain he lives in the Midlands." He licks his lips habitually in the time-honoured tradition of those dry-throated and parched due to the prolonged intake of skunk-weed and cheap cider. "If we split the letters up we have the possibility of two words: 'ong' and 'itch'. What if she missed some letters in her panic? What if she was trying to sign the word long?" James types in 'long itch', adds Midlands place names as a base guide and clicks search.

And there it was: Long Itchington, a small village some nine or ten miles up the A423 from Coventry.

I knew we had it. I knew it in my bones, my water, every atom and nuclei.

I know exactly where the village is, for I have travelled these dark back-roads a hundred times, eyes red and burning from looking past hedgerows into fields and woods, looking for something – anything – that might ease my aching frustration.

I go back to my files. To the exhaustive study we had made years earlier of hardware stores and builders merchants, searching for a possible supplier of all the ply-wood and plaster-board the killer must have bought to construct his fiendish maze.

Yet again the facts leap out at me. Every piece of the jigsaw falling into place.

A store in Southam had sold a large quantity of materials to a man who lived in a run-down house some two miles down a single-track road not far from the quiet village of Napton, a stone's throw from Long Itchington. The man's name was Terrence Blanck. He had been interviewed but eventually discounted when he provided a plausible reason for the purchases. But several detectives at the time, including myself, had never been entirely satisfied. He had been watched for several weeks, even followed for a while. But when it became obvious that his profession as a plasterer accounted for all the materials he had bought, and when no further evidence could be found, my superiors instructed that we concentrate our efforts elsewhere.

In a single bound I grab my coat and am out the door, yelling over my shoulder as I go: "Call the station! Tell them: Terrence Blanck! I'll meet them there…." And I'm off.

Which brings me to where I am now. Full circle. What goes around comes around.

I have taken his legs for they have chased and prolonged the torture. I have taken his hands for inflicting the pain. I have taken his tongue for the mocking and his eyes for the enjoyment of witnessing their degradation.

His heart I have taken for myself, left steaming in a shallow pool of icy water. A voice beside me and I turn and look at the young Constable.

"Inspector Cale. Sir." He has an expression of deference but his eyes blaze as if in anticipation of the story he can tell of such monumental events so early in his short career. And with something more, for there is also horror reflected in the paleness of his complexion.

"It's time to go sir."

I nod. I glance at each of my colleagues. They can't look me in the eye. At least they cuffed my hands in front of me. As they lead me away I look back. Just once.

And smile.

# JUSTIN WADE THOMPSON

## How I Buried Jesse James

I buried Jesse James under an old pecan tree
behind the house
        where I lived as a child.

I pulled pages from an old book, folded and torn.

I used them, like a shovel
to dig into the brown earth, while Jesse's eyes
turned black

like the eyes of
a sparrow
and
    he growled and snarled and spit, foaming
at the mouth.

my brothers and sisters sat with their backs
against the house
            against the red bricks
in the ferns
like brown spider children
while my old Cherokee grandfather
waxed his '56 Chevy, in the drive way

smiling in his mind, about the Japs he'd skinned
in the Pacific.
Jesse skinned and scalped men, in his day
just like my grandfather
        murdered merrily, under the mask of the red
rising sun.

my pockets were full of tulips, when I came
running back

from Jesse's grave.
my brothers
and sisters
      mocked me, and threw rocks
across the yard
and chewed on grains of sand.

I ran to my grandfather, and pulled a tulip
out from my trousers

and he screamed at me.

DON'T EVER DO THAT AGAIN he said, It's like pulling
a gun on someone, or turning a knife
at the dinner table.

I was sorry for what I'd done, though
I didn't fully understand

and watched the tulip fall to the ground
as if it were a teardrop
      falling from heaven.

# THE TOLEDO PENIS READER

## Tom Badyna

I had my drinks and made to leave. Eve, the bartender, looked up from her boys at the bar's far end and said "Where'd'ya think yer going?"

I said, "Home," and she said, "Ya better be here tomorrow, Badyna."

"Why's that?"

"Because we're having a penis reader."

She said it without missing a beat, but I knew better than to act as if I believed her, whether I did or not. I raised my hand, palm out, in farewell, and went out the door and home where I had an email from Geller which I begged off properly answering for another night, claiming I had had a drink too many. He wrote back immediately to chide me that as tomorrow was Halloween I'd be in the bar, all night, getting trashed and hooking up. I wrote back that I didn't do that, not like he thought, but didn't know that I could pass up the bar's Halloween as they were having the famous Toledo penis reader for the occasion.

He wrote that I was lying, and I wrote that I wasn't. Didn't New York have penis readers?

He said that I was still lying.

I said her name was Sophie, and she used to read palms, but found that penises paid better.

He wrote, Really?

I wrote, Yes, and he asked if I was going to have my penis read.

I said, Probably not, and he wrote that I'd better go early and get in line and give him a full report, all the details. He said he'd send me whatever it cost. He'd Western Union it, if necessary.

This is true.

Geller, I hadn't seen in ten years, but for a couple of years, the coming-of-age years, we were Heckle and Jeckle, and you get only one friendship like that. With a little attention, you keep it all your life, even if one goes on to a married life with children, a job climbing positions in newspapers – reporter, columnist, ombudsman, managing editor all with a corresponding progression of domiciles, apartment, condo, townhouse, a brick Tudor in Riverdale with a swing set – and the other one doesn't.

But I didn't stop in the bar after work. It was Halloween, and after a day stacking rock in the cold and wind, three thousand pounds a pallet, nine pallets a day, I liked my own stool, with some elbow room, and not so much of a crowd of yahoos forcing fun. I didn't know if Eve was lying or not, and didn't care and drove past the bar and around the corner home to my portion of a shithole triplex and, with a slow drink in one hand, all the lights out so as to keep away trick-or-treaters, pecked out on the keyboard a woman, Sophie. She'd studied in Paris, palm reading, but wasn't no good at it. She came home to Toledo where the second of her many fiancés suggested, in an intimate moment and maybe as a joke, that she ought to read penises, as truth would not only be entirely beside the point, but borderline unethical. And though Sophie dismissed the idea, then began the dreams, gauzy instructional videos, as it were. These her fiancé wanted to know all about, and when he repeatedly tried to talk her into trying out her knew knowledge on his friends, she grew angry enough to do it – and found that she was suddenly scary accurate.

I wrote that and, seven in the morning, leaving for work, I hit Send. Five o'clock, I stopped in the bar and told Eve that my friend in New York wanted to know all about the penis reader.

She said I should've been there. Her crowd of boys echoed her.

"You got your dick read, Linus?" I said.

"It took her an hour," he said.

"To what? Find it?"

I took my drink and went to the bar's far end and sat and looked down the galley way to the tragedy of Eve's big feet. She had on low-top Converse sneakers, black, with yellow laces. They were boats. Hard to exaggerate. Size thirteen would have been a reasonable guess, maybe a polite one. She had hands to match, but she was a tall girl and had long gangling arms with a tomboy's grace, and her fingers were long and slender and kinda sexy to contemplate as they wrapped lightly around glasses and bottles. Feet, though, no matter how slender, were another matter.

Eve, daughter of a Hungarian mother and something else and from East Toledo – a side of town out of which nothing had ever come that anyone remembered but car thieves, crack heads and bricklayers – was, at fifteen sent to Paris, by her mother, to be a model. This was never talked about, not in the bar, not otherwise either, what had happened with all that. She was twenty-seven, married to a friend of mine, a man fifteen years her senior. At their home, on an end table squeezed between an over-stuffed, blue couch -- which, anytime I had ever seen it, looked like someone had stayed up to dawn on it, watching TV, smoking dope, gauging the cultural moment -- there were a few framed photos from Eve's Paris go. Small, unadvertised. Cluttered up with ordinary pictures.

That's how it was in Toledo.

You put yourself out there, did something to separate yourself from the herd, and no one gave a fuck. Not unless you came back. And then they didn't give a fuck but that you came back. Proof that what's out there wasn't so special.

Art Tatum, maybe the greatest jazz pianist ever, certifiably the fastest anyway, came out of Toledo and went to New York and outplayed everyone in Harlem by his lonesome, and came back to Toledo to visit family and wander out at night to what was left of the black, jazz dives where he'd started. He'd sit in on a few sets without announcement and leave without fanfare, and people'd say, "That brother can play," and someone'd go, "That was Art Tatum," and someone else'd say, "Well, he can shore play." And someone else'd add, "And he shore can drink, too."

That's how it was in Toledo.

Daws Butler, the voice of Yogi Bear, Wally Gator, Huckleberry Hound, Quick Draw McGraw and Elroy Jetson – which, in aggregate, was a fair estimation of how the Toledo of his boyhood sounded – went to California and never came back and no one wondered why. The voice of Yogi Bear wouldn't mean much in a town where half the population had an uncle who sounded the same.

Joe E. Brown, Danny Thomas, Petroleum V. Nasby, P. J. O'Rourke, Gloria Steinem, Toledoans all – they never came back. Their shtick wouldn't stand out. Eugene Kranz, the flight-director hero of Apollo 13 as played by Ed Harris – what would he have done back in Toledo? Jim Parker, second greatest offensive tackle in football history – what? Jan Roberts, an actually memorable Playboy centerfold, August 1962? Tom Scholz, founder of rock band Boston, Lyman Spitzer Jr., theoretical physicist and driving genius behind the Hubble telescope – gone, gone and gone, as was Marty Frankel, the great embezzler, though he had an excuse involuntary and ironclad, as did Ernie McSorley, captain of the Edmund Fitzgerald.

Edith Church, famed organizer of nudist colonies in the 1930s and '40s, an intellectual, a gifted piano teacher and flamboyant pioneer of interracial love, she stayed. But only until Toledo burned down her house, June 1951. Incinerated its legendary living room with her twin, gleaming grand pianos at which had played Paul Robeson, Eugene Debs, Irving Howe, Sinclair Lewis, Artur Rubinstein and a thousand students, my dad included. It was as if New Yorkers had got it in their heads to torch the round table at the Algonquin.

It was a funny little city.

Mildred Benson, author of the Nancy Drew books – she stayed and stayed and lived freaking forever, but no one gave a fuck.

Paul Timman, Hollywood's tattoo artist of choice, didn't like to admit to Toledo. Anita Baker tried to change her birth certificate – to Detroit. Janet Cooke, the Washington Post journalist star who won a Pulitzer for reporting on an eight-year-old junkie she'd made up, had her threads unravel when she was caught fabricating autobiographical detail. She was surprised – surprised that anyone in Toledo had bothered to call her out.

Katie Holmes, though, she returned. She showed up at the bar I'm talking about. Showed up for a band, as the bar, though small and cheap and mostly a righteous drinking establishment, had a rep for hip bands starting out. That was my friend's doing, Eve's husband. You make the turn for forty and look in the mirror, see a guy with a cigarette distributorship, a yacht-club wife, and clumsy ballerina daughters, and if you can see the truth and turn in the keys to it all, you buy a dump of a bar and make yourself an aficionado of unknown bands, give them a venue and keep it that way. Small, tawdry and hip. You get to marry the Eve's of the world, even with a name like Rupert. Lollipop Lust Kill had got their start at Rupert's Bar, and Katie Holmes showed up in a limousine, with some Hollywood friends. She was gonna show 'em her Toledo. Linus, working the door to pay his tab, carded them. One member of Katie Holmes' entourage hadn't I.D and Linus told her she wasn't getting in.

Katie said, "She's with me."

Linus said, "I don't give a fuck. She ain't getting in"'"

"Then I'll leave," said Mrs. Tom Cruise.

Linus said, "So go already."

True story.

And that's Toledo.

And Eve, like Sophie, had come back, but without a trade. Her feet were too big, a subject, at times, talked about with the rough humor of our class. Paris, though, never was. And neither were the looks she had, the kind that could make a two-year go of Paris while all the world but Toledo hoped her clown feet and oak tree ankles shrank.

I'd come back too, from New York, long before. A subtler tragedy.

I sat at my end of the bar and watched Eve and didn't like how she was with her fan club of little boys there every day for all the after-work hours. She had to be banging one, some, or all of them. I had my guesses. Linus, of course. They had something special, whatever it was, and whatever it was, I didn't want to figure it. Younger than she, Linus had the beard and blond dreadlocks and expertise –a small, nowhere job, printing bumper stickers – of one who attains indisputable rooster cool by being nothing, putting himself out not an inch, not about anything.

There was him, and then there was big, round-headed Charlie, a purebred mystery, the kind of guy whose own eyes knew he was the mope who died on Omaha beach, got senselessly head-onned by a sleepy semi, had a genetically programmed myocardial infarction at thirty-five. He wasn't gonna let you in so as you didn't feel so bad when he bought it. If Eve was gonna fuck around on Rupert, you could see that she could excuse herself for doing it with Charlie. I could. Six drinks in and I half-wanted to fuck Charlie. He had that effect. He played his grandpa's ukulele in his spare time and had an N.B.A. sex life.

And then there was Schroeder, a five-foot-five squirrel boy. Hyper and half-schooled in computers, he played the role of being smarter than the rest, but since he wasn't, he had to feel bad and modest about being so, which both made his smarts seem more real and gave him this suppressed anger, as he would have been obviously seen, with any other skill, as the box of rocks he was. He was the unlikeliest of squeezes for Eve, but he made her laugh, his anger did, when it peeked out, so irrationally vituperative and ridiculous was it. I could see her, drunk enough, letting him have at it. No doubt, Schroeder would have been an industrious, busy fuck, probably a sick one, too. He claimed that when a girl was starting to come he liked to stick a thumb up her ass, cut off that orgasm shit, change the tone, get her mad and hungry and real. He claimed that and worse. You could see him finished, standing up his naked hundred and twenty flyweight pounds, ready to go again, and if Eve slurred a demurral, he might spit on her. You could see it. And that act, the spitting, so ridiculous, a Schroeder spitting on an Eve, might, a week or so down the line, get him another go. You could see it.

The fourth was Woodstock, hair in his eyes, beak nose, all his life in the fraternity of Delta Omega Loser and not minding it so much, not yet, and I sat at my end of the bar and watched Eve and didn't like how she was with her fan club and didn't know if she liked it that I always sat at the far end of the bar. I had my drinks enough for All Saints Day and went home to an email from Geller.

He wasn't interested in the proofreading work he had outsourced to me. He wanted to know if I had had my penis read. My email hadn't said. And he wanted to know. He wanted to know how she did it. "Details, man," he wrote, "details." Did she hold it in her hands? Did she look close? Did she read the veins and wrinkles? What happened if it started erecting? What did she forecast? Your sex life? Your whole life? What? "If you're going to be a writer, you need to get the details. The reader needs to know if Sophie made a prediction on the future of Tommy's pee-pee."

I could see Geller in his Riverdale study with its French doors closed against his family, slurping the cheap beers he favored as a matter of principle and picked out like one would a pair of distressed jeans. I could see his hundred and forty kosher pounds quivering against the genetic ambition that jailed him, unable to help his vicarious salivating.

I wanted to reply, "Fuck you," but, instead, wrote, "What's between a man and his penis reader is privileged," and hit Send and turned off the computer, and next morning read Geller's accusation that I had chickened out, hadn't had the brass to get my penis read. As a favor to my character, he wrote, Western Union had forty dollars for me. If I didn't go hand it over to Sophie, he'd lose all respect for me.

I pushed the forty across the bar and asked Eve for details, and she said that the penis reader didn't exist. "That's not exactly true," I said and told her about Geller and Sophie and Paris palm reading, and she got it, got it all, had her captivated and laughing with an acumen I had previously suspected.

Her fanboys at the far end watched me hold her attention and mumbled about, mouths agape. Without Eve to hear, they didn't hardly have anything to say.

Eight o'clock came, and, her shift over, Eve moved 'round the bar to sit next to me, and the boys came down awkward, which was exactly why I had never stayed to eight o'clock – so as not to see what happened at eight o' five. Eve, embarrassed, told the boys she wasn't going tonight, and we talked, Eve and I, first time in three years, really talked, heads hung together, shoulders now and again leaned into each other like warm volts of electricity we couldn't stand too long.

"You have to tell your friend the truth," she said.

"It's the most fun I've had in years," I said.

And nine o'clock, pudgier than the last time I'd seen him, Rupert came in, to be there for the band's first night ever, to make sure they showed, existed. Purportedly, they were a group from the sixty-mile-away University of Michigan, from its big-deal music school. They wanted the occasional break from Tchaikovsky, play a little cash-earning funk. Rupert was pretty excited about having them and moved about the bar, cash register, phone, stage, this customer and that. "One guy, from Toledo, is a genius, I think," we heard him say, and Eve and I, couldn't tell if he was first taking care of business so as to later give us proper attention, or was avoiding us. With her head angled down, Eve's eyes followed Rupert. She seemed sad. We didn't talk, and Rupert came over, and I said, "I got the greatest practical joke ever going," and he nodded, gave a half smile. "The Toledo Penis Reader," I said. "That's great," he said. His eyes darted to Eve. She shook her head.

"What're ya drinking, Rupe?" I said. He said nothing. He and Eve were looking at each other, and they were trying to half-smile. I went home and wrote Geller all about the famous Toledo Penis Reader, that there's no danger of an erection because as she's holding your cock, she's seeing truth, and it hurts.

And next day I didn't go to the bar, after work, and Geller had written in the middle of his work day that he had talked to a friend of his, the editor for Maxim Magazine, and got himself assigned to come to Toledo, expenses paid, to write a feature on Miss Sophie.

Nathan Geller couldn't just come write the story. He couldn't do it without the imprimatur of an official assignment and one only from a magazine as legit as Maxim. I wrote that he could pocket the expense money and stay with me.

And he wrote that he knew how I lived and might I recommend a hotel and then added, "Nevermind." He did so without deleting the bit about me recommending a hotel because it was funny not to delete it, to say "nevermind' instead. He would call me a week from Tuesday, when he got in. I might make an appointment for him that Wednesday, with Miss Sophie. And then he added, "Nevermind," to that. Just send him her phone number.

And I told Eve.

And she said I had to tell him.

And Linus, Charlie, Schroeder, Woodstock – they came down to my end of the bar. "Let's do it, man," they said. "It'll be fucking great."

"And who's gonna be the fucking penis reader?" said Eve, and when everyone laughed, looked at her, she added, looking at Schroeder, "We'll dress up Squirrel Boy here."

"No, man. You gotta do it. You fucking got to."

Eve looked at me, and I wasn't so sure, but the boys were. They were like dogs on a short leash in a biscuit factory.

And in Eve's eyes were obligations.

She gave me her cell number, to give to Geller, but he could only call between eleven and noon. "You owe me, Badyna. Big time." She had kindness in her eyes and was sorry she did.

And Tuesday night, I waited for Geller's call. I'd dressed, done laundry, cleaned the joint up, organized my desk – just in case – so it might look like a writer's, had taken the afternoon off, had three nights in a row reacquainted myself with Toledo's two jazz clubs so I might be treated as a familiar face and be a proper tour guide. I'd gotten half the city in on the joke, it seemed, so that mention of the Toledo Penis Reader would be shrugged off, treated as old hat.

I called the airport. The day's last flight from New York had landed at 5:05. Forty-two years old and I was having the emotional experience of a teenage girl.

A quarter after eleven, Geller called and was sorry and tired and still working on his laptop and we'd go have a beer tomorrow night. He had a Thursday morning flight.

I said I'd taken Wednesday off.

"Can you afford doing shit like that?"

I said I'd pick him up. We'd have breakfast. I'd take him to Sophie's parlor.

He said that on the flight in he'd gotten a sick feeling about this, that it was a mistake, a waste of time. He couldn't write a story about flying to Toledo to have his penis read.

"You're using a pseudonym."

"There's just something wrong with it."

"Remember. You wanted to be Tom Wolfe, Hunter Thompson, James Agee. This is like that. They would do it."

"I don't know."

"You're here, brother."

"You know what's on my screen? I'm three clicks from changing my flight to tomorrow. I lied to my fucking wife."

"What'd'ya tell her?"

"That I'm coming to see you."

Noon I went downtown and picked him up, and we went for burgers and beers. He interviewed me about having my penis read, and, as arranged, I had him call Squirrel Boy, who came down, and though I wasn't so sure that he wouldn't wreck the whole thing, Schroeder rose to the occasion rather brilliantly, talked how he liked to get his penis read at least once a month. You believed him, to see and hear him. I almost believed him.

"Does your penis change month to month?"

"The way I abuse it, it does."

Geller ate it up. He was like Woodward and Bernstein taking it all down. He was like the old Geller, life as an act of discovery, and I was very happy seeing him like this, laughing, curious, and I was very happy that it was me opening the doors to the strange world of Toledo, Ohio, the one nobody knew, not in the bigger world, because no one ever came back. Geller shot me looks now and again. This world was a revelation to him, and I lived in it. He was burning to write for the first time in years and years.

Charlie followed Squirrel Boy as interview subject, and he was perfectly dull and halting enough to be even more believable. "It's not a good future she told me."

"So how many times have you had your penis read?"

"No. That was enough."

And we left for East Toledo, where a fan of Eve's, a friend of Rupert's, had a vacant storefront the boys had transformed into a penis-reading parlor. That morning Linus had put up the signs he'd made at work, and when Geller and I arrived, Linus was out front telling a few passersby they needed an appointment. They pointed at the sign. "Walk-ins Welcome." "It's a fucking sign," Linus told them.

We hurried Geller in, and Woodstock stumbled out from behind the purple curtains like someone had told him his dog had died, which was how he commonly looked at four in the afternoon, and I went across the street to a lesbian biker bar, Rosebud's, and they didn't mind me, not much, not once I passed the test of no consequence. That's how it was in Toledo. Six o'clock Geller came got me. He had a beer.

"How was it?"

"She's freaking beautiful."

"Yeah, but she has big feet."

"She has what? Nevermind. I got a fucking great story. I mean it. If I can write it. I mean, I don't know. There's something here, something real, really real."

He said that and shook my hand and opened his laptop.

"Don't do that."

"What?"

"Open your laptop."

"Why not?"

"Trust me."

"Why not?"

"Just don't."

He laughed and nodded and looked 'round the bar. "I love Toledo, man. This – I mean, you're missing the boat. This is a writer's paradise."

"So what'd Sophie say? Does little Nathan got a good future."

"Man, it's private."

He said that and shook my hand again and talked earnest, about me, advice, earnest advice he gave me in his Geller way, like last wise words. Then we got drunk, old Geller and I, in a lesbian biker bar called Rosebud's in East Toledo, a part of town out of which nothing had ever come but car thieves, crackheads and bricklayers, and we were of no consequence, not enough so they'd mind and I didn't mind the advice this time. I wasn't gonna take it, but I didn't mind it then and there, where, boy-o-boy, was it good to drink with my old friend. Next day, after work, I was at Rupert's. I gave Eve the news and she said, "You can't let him publish it."

"If I tell him, our friendship's over."

"Your friendship's over anyway."

"What'd'ya mean?"

"I foretold it."

I looked at her.

"Look," she said. "You don't see him for ten years. He travels and never stops to see you. But to have a stranger look at his dick, for that he comes to Toledo."

"But we were, you know. He knows a side of me no one else does."

"You have to tell him," she said and put her cell phone on the bar.

---

"Eve, think about it. The Toledo Penis Reader. This is big. Maxim Magazine. I mean it'll go Letterman, Leno. This is the freaking greatest practical joke since the Plainfield Teachers College, back in the '30 – "

Eve looked unknowing, unconcerned with knowing.

"This is turning the tables. It's justice. They're always looking down on us. It's so fucking classic, and we've done it. I'm not calling."

I said that and looked at Linus, whom I was sitting next to. "Call," he said.

And Squirrel Boy – "Call," he said.

And Charlie nodded and said, "Call."

And Woodstock nodded like someone had told him his dog had died.

And I said, "He feels like a writer for the first time in forever. You guys have no idea what that means."

Eve shook her head and a few weeks later an editor at Maxim Magazine called her cell to verify the story.

# NO MORE JOHNSONS

## Michael Fedo

More than 700 members of the Johnson Cognomen Confederacy, representing all 50 states and Puerto Rico, met yesterday in Dick Johnson Township, Indiana, to discuss how to get Americans not named Johnson to stop referring to the male appendage as a Johnson.

Confederacy founder A. R. Johnson told reporters that Johnson is the second most popular surname in the country and is shared by millions of hard-working, decent citizens. "These good people should not be subject to continued opprobrium because years ago, some unknown wag thought he was being droll," Mr. Johnson said. "We Johnsons have endured this derisive advertence for decades, and it's time to call a halt."

Mr. Johnson (hereinafter referred to as A. R. as other Johnsons are cited in this article) added that he also would take no satisfaction should the long-established childhood monikers Peter or Willy gain greater eminence among adults—whether or not they are Johnsons. "I enjoy a bit of humor as much as the next man," he said. "But we need to be more circumspect with our priapic allusions."

Emil Johnson, a bar owner from Orrock, Minnesota, claims history is replete with notable Johnsons whose name has been tarnished with the appellation. "May I remind you that two U. S. Presidents, Andrew and Lyndon, were Johnsons."

"Plus there's the foundation of Robert Wood Johnson," A. R. added. "And we have the safari folks, Martin and Osa Johnson, baseball's Randy, literature's Samuel and Ben. And let me say that while old Ben spelled his name without the h, the h is silent so who cares? In another direction there's Liver Eating Johnson, who doesn't merit regard for anything except his infamy, and of course the excellent film Jeremiah Johnson, based on him, starring Robert Redford. I'd be remiss in not mentioning the well-known Johnson & Johnson enterprise, and the great Olympian Rafer Johnson, who has had a junior high school named for him.

"Oh, I bet you didn't know that Whoopi Goldberg is also a Johnson. She was born Caryn Elaine Johnson. And everyone knows of Howard, the motelier and restaurateur. Told Americans everything they needed to know about ice cream. All these and many more. My point: there are countless noteworthy Johnsons, and each time the body part is

Johnsonized, it impugns the character of every Johnson past, present and future. We want this issue rectified sooner than later."

LeRoy Johnson-Johnson, an alternative systems analyst from Delaware Water Gap, Pa., stated he hyphenates his last name in homage to both his mother's Johnsons and his father's Johnsons. "It's my way of showing pride in the Johnson name, letting folks know that both my parents were Johnsons and proud descendants of Johnsons," he said.

"I was among the many boys of my generation who called the dangler a peter. That was until a lad named Peter Johnson was in my seventh grade geography class. The kid was mercilessly teased. Never knew a Willy Johnson, but my half-brother Ralf did." LeRoy sighed.

"Every time roll is taken in schoolrooms nationwide, and the name Peter Johnson or Willy Johnson is announced, other kids smirk. The conundrum is compounded when those chaps are either over or under-endowed. For the sake of all of us who bear the Johnson name I implore my fellow countrymen to desist."

Meanwhile, Darwin L. Johnson, a retired mortician from Washington Court House, Ohio, holds an alternative view. A candidate for a seat on the Johnson Cognomen Confederacy board, Darwin says, "I've been a Johnson all my life, which is 70-plus years and would bring a lot of Johnson experience to the job, and maybe get them to rethink this notion." He said he joined the Confederacy last April following a divorce. "I thought it would be a nice way to meet an available lady of my approximate age with matrimony in mind. And it would be easier for this lady if she needn't consider a name change upon remarriage. But if she marries another Johnson—no problem.

"Actually I've never felt maligned about this Johnson business. I think many of us are amused if not honored by the reference. On the other hand my former wife's nickname for my thingamajig was Mr. Fitzsimmons, which is what I came to call it myself. But if the confederacy feels a change is absolutely necessary, how about Mr. Fitzsimmons replacing the shopworn Johnson? My ex would be all for it, and I wouldn't mind myself."

The discussion continued throughout the day with other Johnsons suggesting further titles. Brenda Johnson, a blogger from Peru, New York, argued that rather than trying to get citizens to cease their whimsical citations, the confederacy itself should take up the cudgel as articulated by the former Mrs. Darwin L. Johnson and start using Mr. Fitzsimmons. "For one thing, it'll take years for those Irish folks to get organized and come up with a different name. Second, I know my husband Earl, who's not present, would enjoy the diminutive 'Mr. Fitzsimmons.' I didn't mean to imply that his Mr. Fitzsimmons is diminutive, however. Far from it."

Kaptain Kielbasa and King Ohyeah gained support among those who believed proper names should not be considered as replacements for the Johnson.

Before the convention adjourned to a catered spread at a Holiday Inn in nearby Terre Haute, a vote was taken. Mr. Fitzsimmons received the majority of ballots cast.

A middle-aged male Johnson who preferred anonymity, said, "I'll do my part, and insinuate Mr. Fitzsimmons into as many casual conversations as possible. I feel confident that if everyone here does the same, the public will come to accept the Fitzsimmons. Then hey, it ain't your grandpa's Johnson anymore."

# CARL MILLER DANIELS

## I think he said his name was "Lucky"

for his halloween costume,
the sexy big-dicked young man decided
to go naked. in other words, he decided he'd
"dress up" as a nudist.
this thought amused the sexy big-dicked young man
very much,
and, the first door he knocked on,
a young woman answered.
"trick or treat," said
the sexy naked big-dicked young man.
he held out a little brown paper sack,
and waited for his treat.
the young woman slammed the door in his face.
he turned and walked down the sidewalk.
very soon, a police car showed up.
two cops hurried over to the
sexy naked big-dicked young man,
and one of the cops wrapped a blanket
around him.
"you're under arrest," said the cop who
had wrapped him up with the blanket.
"indecent exposure."
"but it's halloween," said the
sexy naked big-dicked young man,
"and this is my costume. i'm 'dressed
up' as a nudist. get it?"
and then the young man
laughed, quite charmingly.
"yeah yeah," said the other cop. "very funny.
but you're STILL under arrest for indecent exposure."
and so the two cops and the sexy big-dicked young man
who was wrapped up in the blanket
drove to the police station/jail.
they booked the sexy big-dicked young man
and issued him some jail clothes and
put him a cell and told him to

get dressed.
the sexy big-dicked young man
refused. in fact, he threw off the blanket,
and stood there sexy, naked, big-dicked,
with a full horny erection that suddenly looked,
in fact, like it was made entirely out of
bone, and then encrusted with
brittle knobby chunks of tortoise shell.
there then ensued what seemed to be
a general melting and fusing of flesh,
and the creature that
the sexy naked big-dicked young man
had become kicked out the bars
of the cell's window, unfurled
a pair of wings, and flew off into the
starry night-time sky.
"happy halloween," were the parting words
the two cops heard, as the goosebumps
seized them, and covered their
pale municipal flesh.

# BARRY SPACKS

## The Letter

I wrote 206 words today, took
22,000 breaths of air
and released every one of them
back to the Commons.

I ate various creatures with my white teeth
smiled twice meaningfully, 83 times for sake of diplomacy,
fell in love with my usual ration, 9,
and tried manfully to keep this letter brief,

but mainly I need to mention my insight
that death itself is perfectly safe,
you can give yourself there with all your might
off we go, unendable ride.

Plus also I washed the dishes twice
managed to let 7 heart-knots slip,
did daily stuff, cat's dish, quip,
wended my way by Thy Will Be Done.

I endured odd thoughts that arrive for no reason,
tried out some goodnesses, played the prick,
all on one day, and thought of you
and of you, and you. And sat like a mountain.

# GENTLEMAN, SCHOLAR

## Zachary Amendt

Wake up crying, real actual tears, the sunlight pouring in, the trees a maw of hungry crows. I'm an easy cry. The doctors don't know what's wrong. My pallor is changing. My liver is oversized. What was it Robert Lowell said, It's not death I fear, but unspecified, unlimited pain. I'm trying to reclaim my mind. Mornings like this I get a flash of cognizance, brief as a pulse-stroke, right as I open my eyes to the world … I say to myself, Salvati, how nice it is to wake up in your own bed. How pleasant. And I find myself in a waterbed in a room with high ceilings; instead of curtains, long vintage dresses are hung on the windows, billowing like the gowns of ghosts. My legs are tangled in the sheets and the waves and an arm is draped over me, bare, hinged to a taut breast, and long hair that's a mess of tangled, dishwater blonde. Tierney is one of my better teaching assistants. I can hear my mind snapping its fingers … this is her parents' vacation home. It's a Sunday and term papers are due in two weeks. Her face is marked from the bedding. There's ink on her lower back. Her lip is pierced.

In the WC there's vomit on the rim of the toilet. Another one of my assistants, Darren, is sleeping on the bathroom floor, cocooned in a comforter he must have dragged off our bed. The commons room looks like a brothel – bodies are strewn about like after Ypres. From the looks of it, we drank yesterday like furloughed prisoners-of-war. Empty Schnapps bottles in the sink. Castles of cups on the ping-pong table. I started a pot of coffee and assumed the thinker's posture on the dining room table, and search me, I couldn't piece last night together if I tried.

\*\*\*

We caravanned upstate in Volkswagens, a who's who of Tierney's "hometeam": the Aggie outfielders Sean and Brock, myself, Darren, Tierney and a litter of her girlfriends, Sharon and Celia and Gabrielle, her on-and-off boyfriend Jones, and three girls named Zoe. She collected loved ones like they were baseball cards.

First thing, Tierney walked around the house pulling sheets off of furniture. She wanted everyone to be comfortable.

"We can make the place up with flowers if you'd like," she assured Jones. "There's nothing flowers can't do."

Jones stood in the open doorway taking in deep draughts of the clean air. He looked out into the woods beyond the low stone fence. In his mind he was flying down country roads, fishing on docks with his feet in the water and crickets squirming between his fingers.

"I want to chop down a tree," he said.

"Not on my property," said Tierney.

It was two or three past noon. The Zoes were angling for booze. Early drinking is only for the stouthearted. We drove to a watering hole in town, Dawson's, with walls festooned with dollar bills and polaroids of regulars holding up fish and game, smiling. The construction workers at the bar were as interesting to the girls as foreigners. One of them was in a Caltrans vest. Another advertised a pool cleaning business on the back of his shirt. Saturday was Independence Day and they were watching a broadcast of last year's fireworks show. After each explosion, the pool guy said:

"There goes $1,000."

I laid $100 down on the bar and we all drank on that, gossiped and took turns feeding the jukebox. Young people are lifting to the spirit. My colleagues, chloroformed by academia, sit around and debate the merits of obscure papers over glasses of imported wines. But I like to drink where Budweiser is king.

I was looking at the grout in the floor tiles when Tierney sidled up next to me. Behind her two of the Zoes were learning to throw darts. The third was watching the boys play billiards.

"How's college?" I said.

"You don't learn anything in college," she said. "You drink in college. You stay up late. I'm 21, but I feel 30, my skin's sallow. I look 30. You learn about men. You learn about cause and effect." She bit at the inside of her cheek. "You find out that people don't need full moons to act like lunatics." Her guts were spilling. "Jones and I are a mess. The mixed tape I made for him he did not acknowledge. I spritz perfume on my love letters. I tell him about lacrosse and my chemistry classes. It only vaguely interests him."

I offered her the Parliament I had bummed from Caltrans. "Plus he calls me disparaging names," she said.

"Like what?"

"'Pile of words.'"

I laughed. "Well, you don't look thirty," I said. "You do look like you haven't been fucked in months."

"Don't say that. You're too old to say that."

"I'm not allowed to say fuck?"

"It's just … vulgar, coming from you."

Tierney, what this friendship means to me. The lengths I would go to. The favors I would renounce. The invitations I would refuse. All in the name of your company and your grace.

\*\*\*

Tierney stirs my rolodex of memories. She reminds me of when I had Georgia and a bungalow in Venice, playing gigs in honkytonks to make rent. Georgia's father had opened up a chain of restaurants across California called The Mad Greek. He invested in developing towns. Our first date was on a Thursday night. I picked her up in an orange Plymouth Roadrunner, a convertible with a four-track player in the console.

What I would not give to have that car today.

"Georgia tells me you're quite the guitarist," her father said. He gave me a firm handshake.

Back then I thought nothing of my talents. "It's a hobby, really," I said.

"What is it you do for a living?"

I had my hands in my pockets. "I work at the phone company," I said.

"What ideas do you have for my daughter tonight, Dennis?"

"Sir, I thought I'd take her to La Talpa and then to the Boardwalk and back to my place.

"To talk," I clarified.

"And what time are you bringing her back?"

"What time do you want her back, sir?"

"Daughter, when do you want Mr. Salvati to drop you off?"

Georgia batted her eyes at him. "Sunday night, Dad."

We dated forever. She made me work for it. I who had nothing … I would have gladly bankrupted myself for her. In the winter we smoked cigars in fingerless gloves and peacoats. Daytrips to Santa Barbara. In a journal we recorded the names of restaurants and meals and rated the looks of the waitresses.

"You should stop smoking," I said.

"I'll stop smoking when all I can taste is the heat," she said.

It shouldn't have gone on as it did, for as long as it did, but thank God it did. And here I sit in rural California in a big sweater the color of toothpaste, drinking weak coffee, waiting for the co-eds to wake. Big shot academic. We were in among the vines of a winery when I proposed to Georgia, blurting it out as one would a baseball score. It was less out of love and more out of desperation. There was so much to remember. Did she smile when she let me down, did she laugh? That's another thing I'm glad I've forgotten.

***

In the parking lot, because I seem the soberest, I'm thrown the keys. It's a Vanagon that, loaded with undergrads, nearly scrapes the ground. The wind is whipping drifts of sand across the road. It seems no-one traverses these outer highways. I wonder with what measure of nostalgia that people born out here look back on these wide open spaces, these infinite vistas. My own childhood was urbane, compacted … Jews in pawn shops discussing the Negro question, morning calisthenics on 200-year-old rugs.

Jones' head was on Tierney's shoulder. He had drunk himself well out of contention. "How are you feeling, Professor?" he asked, thickly. His tongue and lips were leaden. Darren was beside him, fully passed out.

I said, "I feel like the Germans who conquered France just to visit its towns."

"He meant are you okay to drive?" It was Gabrielle. She resembled Charlotte Rampling. I've seen Gaby pour barefoot into taxicabs at 5 a.m., holding her high heels, with stamps on her hands and wristbands. Girls like her make me pine for the old American morality, where one was ostracized for one highball too many at lunch, or cheating at golf.

"Aye," I replied.

"I've heard all about you," said Gaby. "I heard you were the best mental exercise on campus."

"I hate it when my students talk in metaphors."

"How's this quarter been for you?" she pressed.

"The worst," I said. "It's because of the election. Y'all have lost your minds."

"I'd like to hear you lecture," Gaby said. She turned to the blonde Zoe. "What I like especially about older men is the grey hair." She reached over and stroked the back of my neck. "It calms me."

"I wasn't always an academic," I said.

46

"No?"

"Some years ago I was a musician."

"You were?" Celia asked. "What happened?"

"I got the wrong gigs," I said.

Gabrielle reached down her blouse to readjust the little that was inside her bra. Her mascara was smeared.

"Then I stopped getting gigs," I said.

I looked again in the rearview at the best and brightest of what is supposed to be the next greatest generation.

"Then I stopped altogether," I said.

\*\*\*

By 9 p.m. everyone was rested up for the evening's drinking. We played games and had a grand old time. At some point Tierney lifted her eyes to me. She was nearsighted and her glasses were not unsightly. She took them off, put them on my face and said:

"You know, professor. Eyeglasses can change your whole outlook."

Or I'm imagining it. I kissed her. Audacity pays dividends. An hour later she was so drunk I had to help her out of her jewelry. It wasn't chivalrous, but once Jones passed out I added Tierney to my repertoire.

At my age, desire gets old.

Fulfillment never gets old.

# ALLISON KADE

## Polaroids

A Polaroid stood upright against the leg of the nightstand, impossibly straight, as though it were a pillar in a house of cards. Another appeared in the kitchen in the girl's green mug, which, luckily, was not full. Photographs hid in the slow remembrance of the dusty, forgotten dictionary—the red one in the back that only came in handy once a year—and they reveled in the sudden shock of being found. One of the gladdest snapshots was a slip of memory in the freezer on top of the cookie dough ice cream. One of the saddest was a wad of thick, hard paper clogging the toilet's rusty innards. That one was irretrievable, the paper wrinkled and the quick-drying ink smeared.

Photographs hid inside the girl's desk. They attached themselves to the outside of her backpack; she tore them away nervously for fear of being seen.

Growing up, the girl thought that all children went through life accompanied by photographs. When she was nearly ten years old, she listened to her parents debate who had taken the first infamous photo. She didn't understand how they could fail to understand. That was when she concluded that, whether or not the photos were a gift, they were a fact to be kept private.

Photos would often appear when the girl looked at something and thought, I want to remember this moment always. But not always—the photos came when they did. Generally, the girl's communion with the Polaroids took place when she was in a daze, idly chewing the inside of her cheek.

She was generally a quiet girl, but she developed an enemy in high school. On one occasion, a cigarette was found in the girls' bathroom. The whole staff searched for the perpetrator, and the girl wanted nothing more than to implicate her enemy in return for all of the verbal abuse. The girl bit her cheek and imagined the photograph she desired. She waited for her eyes to glaze over, for the mental click, but no matter how hard she tried—no matter that the enemy was probably the true culprit, anyway—the Polaroids took no heed.

The enemy continued to ridicule the girl at school, but a young man began to defend her after he found a Polaroid. Picking it up from the floor near the girl's locker, he stared at it for a long minute before placing it in his own notebook. An aspiring photographer himself, he loved its understated eloquence: mannequins wearing pearls, a thrift shop disco ball. For weeks he continued to defend the girl against her enemy, as he watched and waited to confirm that the photo was really hers. The day of confirmation came when he noticed the girl slip a photograph from her lunch bag into her pocket.

More and more Polaroids began to crop up around school. The young man made it a point to talk to the girl every day, and she reciprocated. When her parents left town for a weekend, they seized the opportunity to be alone. They explored everything about each other through their hands. In the amber haze of skin and hair and fingertips, the girl did not notice the telltale click.

A photo of the young man, blurry with movement, materialized in her mother's dresser drawer. When accused of showing off her disobedience, the girl boiled with indignation at her own subconscious. As though they were in a fight, the photos refused to surface for a week.

Once everything cooled down again, the young man invited the girl to attend the carnival. A photograph of them flying down the rollercoaster (her hair expanded like an amber parachute, his face turned to admire it, as though he knew himself to be posing for posterity) appeared in the girl's purse, and she gave it to him. He was pleased.

Strolling past the candied apples and corn on the cob, she didn't realize at first that he was walking with direction. He led her to a booth run by scouts for a national art contest. When he begged her to submit the photograph, she refused. The young man considered the photo she gave him to be his property and, when she wasn't looking, submitted it anyway.

It won. But when the committee tried to publish it in their magazine, nothing appeared but a gray square. The contest managers nervously concluded that the girl must have had some special reproduction-proof technology to protect her copyright. The committee members phoned the young man; he confessed to them and to her.

Although the girl was angry, she was also secretly pleased. She played along with the copyright excuse. She cited artistic integrity as her reason for having no backup negatives. After word got out that her photos couldn't be replicated, the same magazine did a feature on her. The article catapulted her into the public view, and she was offered her first gallery exhibit.

Perhaps because there were no definitive copies, no one noticed that the snapshots changed over time. Some of the rich art collectors who owned them occasionally noted slight differences from when the photographs were purchased, but the snapshots changed too gradually to be sure. After enough time, one had to swallow his doubts and convince himself that of course a certain figure had always been there, and that while the color might have faded a little, the composition of the shot was still mostly the same. People fooled themselves out of believing that figures in their photos had aged or disappeared, or that the new faces hadn't been there from the start.  It is amazing how little people trust their own memories.

The girl was oblivious at first. She remembered the events behind every photo exactly as they appeared in hard copy. Only when the young man pulled up a chair and placed a photo on her lap did she begin to understand. The photo he had taken at the carnival showed the two of them alongside two other friends. The colors were less vivid, more mundane. The girl's Polaroid made no mention of the classmates. All the same, she smiled and handed it right back. She didn't know what she would do if the young man noticed.

After the first exhibition, she was offered a contract for a traveling showcase and a lecture series. The first time that she stood up on a podium, she nearly laughed at telling others how to take a photograph. By the fourth time, she started to forget that she had never actually taken a photograph herself.

The young man always solicited her opinion on photography, but her preference was to talk about life, music, other things. All the same, she was flattered by the nervous way he spoke around her. He invited her to the opening of someone in his artists' circle. His friends swarmed around her when she arrived. She was pretty, they said, prettier than you'd expect for the photographic voice of their time. The exhibition artist might have been jealous, but he waited to ask her questions all the same.

After graduation, the girl and the young man moved in together. They went for coffee with the artists' circle every day, where the girl fielded questions and indulged in plenty of advice-giving. The group brooded over self-determination and discussed the ironies of modernization over their Colombian brew, black. She enjoyed this.

On the way back to the apartment, the two of them walked past graffitied warehouse facades. Inside, they continued to talk about life and oedipal complexes and the meaning of reincarnation. This developed into a routine, the two of them lying next to each other as they stared at the ceiling. There was nothing else to do, as the caffeine forbade midday sleep.

Throughout this era, the photos changed in style. They used to be a childhood remembered, with figures like sculptures telling a story to the marble halls of a museum. Over time, they became more visceral. The snapshots were no longer Victorian tableaus, but rather impressions that captured emotions. A favorite childhood doll's red lips and strands of polyester hair began to blur in one of her snapshots. The more mature version of the photograph betrayed the carpet stain behind the plastic head and the place where the doll's arm fell off. The image couldn't explain her parents' inability to buy a replacement—but there were echoes.

Collectors marveled at her versatility. The young man was even more obsessed with the girl's critical acclaim than she. While he dedicated himself to perfecting his art—he lived, breathed, photography—the girl stopped monitoring her reviews very closely. She was jealous of the young man's passion for his medium. At times she felt more like a broker.

One afternoon, as she gave in to the warm eddies of his breath against the nape of her neck, she heard a click. The snapshot was waiting behind the coffeemaker. She plucked it out and left it on the young man's dresser.

He loved it. In the image, his head peeked out above the amber ocean of her hair as they lay together, though there was no way she could have gotten the angle by holding the camera herself. The young man did not remember a tripod. The girl considered telling a tale, but she had never told anyone her secret. She wanted someone to say that it was okay, that her gift was beautiful. The young man's arms circled and squeezed her waist.

She told him about the mental snapshots. She told him about her accidental fame and her lack of reproduction-proof technology.

He accused her of being a fake. The photos were a gift that appeared of their own volition, he said. She had no right to take credit; her subconscious was simply splattering itself onto paper. The young man was hurt and also jealous. He said that what she did was like cheating.

The girl hated that he was more upset about her art than about her. She would have understood if he felt betrayed because she had not told him earlier, but that was not his complaint.

She apologized, but he did not accept it. She apologized twice, three times, and then did not apologize anymore. The young man moved out.

The last photo, a scene from their fight, taped itself to her mirror. It depicted the young man's angry lips mid-yell. She ripped it off and filed it in an album. She went around town and squinted. She bit her cheek and waited for the shutter click inside her mind. It didn't come. She kept trying, until the inside of her cheek began to bleed. The photos refused to appear.

Alone in the apartment, she dwelled. After a few weeks that passed in a haze, she finally heard a click again. By the espresso beans lay her first duplicate photo, the scene from the fight. Confused, she placed it in the album alongside the original.

More of them cropped up everywhere. The same photo, over and over, of the young man with a snarl, appeared all over the apartment. Three of them were on the sofa, five of them by the bathtub, and one of them stuffed into the air vent. The girl went through, one by one, filing them into albums. Only upon viewing the thirtieth copy did she realize that each was slightly different. In some, the young man's mouth was a little more ajar, and in others his head was turned a slightly different direction.

They kept multiplying. Strewn all over the floors and countertops, the number increased every day. After two weeks, there was a flood of Polaroids two feet deep. The girl couldn't bathe because Polaroids filled the shower. They burst out of cabinets and fell from the ceiling rafters. Sitting in bed, she was a lonely huddle amid the smell of quick-drying photographic ink.

Around this time, she began to have dreams: some were eerie, some were happy, and some were almost indistinguishable from reality. She awoke to find new duplicates at the top of the giant heap. The more she dreamt, the more photos surfaced. Dozing in and out, she could only half-differentiate the wildest of the dream photos from the others.

In an effort to stem the tide, she went to the store and bought a mechanical camera. She wanted to prove that she was a photographer as much as the young man was, to prove that she was more than a mere art broker. She tried to recapture the magic of her earlier instants, but the device was cold and metallic against her eye. She returned to sites where she had taken snapshots in the past, but the mechanical photos weren't the same.

Faced with the camera, the Polaroids ceased. They relegated themselves to the corners of her vision, hiding in the pink caruncle of her eyes.

Her work with a camera was mediocre at best. Fewer and fewer visitors came to her shows, and the critics supported their boycott. She put aside the Polaroid and bought a fancy photographer's camera with knobs and lenses and a thick instruction booklet that she read end to end. She became obsessed with proving that she could be a legitimate photographer if she tried.

Unfortunately, this was not the case. The critics demanded the Polaroids of old, but she refused, recalling her oft-cited artistic integrity. There was a problem, however: she was no longer new, exciting, or original.

The girl continued to take mediocre photographs of things like flowers and babies for many years. She saved only one copy of her last snapshot—the image of the young man's last angry second of their relationship—in the bottom of a drawer that she never opened. As time passed, the expression of the man who looked out shifted from a scowl to a sad smile of understanding. She might have noticed this and understood the change in her own feelings, visible in the gradual softening of his face and the nostalgia that filled the small Polaroid square. But he had never called her, and she never looked at the photo again.

She hung the other Polaroids on the wall in neat little frames. They were miniature reminders of what was, and, if she so chose, the flood that could be unleashed again.

She died in her sleep many years later, at an age that was neither young nor old but perfectly respectable. As she slept on her last night, her will finally broke. One more Polaroid appeared on her nightstand. It was confused, blurry, and dark. A few minutes later, that photo, the gallery of frames, and every Polaroid purchased by every art collector, flashed suddenly into gray squares.

# JOHN GROCHALSKI

## Worst agonies

some days
the worst agonies
are typical things
like missing the train
after sitting through a meeting
or watching a stranger
smile at a child.

it is standing in line
for a jar of gravy
behind someone with
a cartload of shit
as the cashier talks on
her cellular phone
as people talk about
the cover stories
on celebrity magazines
and you realize that it
takes so much effort
to sound so common.

it is watching a baseball game
in october, drunk,
with the lights off
and the workday hours away
it is getting political pamphlets
in the mail
or waiting on the sun to shine
after another bout of insomnia.

the worst agonies

are so simple and precise
a broken stoplight
a lost pen
losing a page in a book
a job interview
the way shadows fall
on the next ugly block
that you must tread toward
your own personal hell
it is hoping to win
but knowing always that
you will lose
it is realizing that death is actual
and that poetry rarely pays the bills.

some days
the worse agonies
come from just having to say hello.
the worst agonies
come from smiling at a neighbor
or just getting out of bed.

and those are the days
my friends
that you're happy
you don't own a gun
you're scared of heights
and that the oven
is electric
and not gas

# TIM HAWKINS

## The Great Depression

During one of those years
about all I owned

was an old black raincoat,
as thin and cheap
and reeking of smoke

as barroom laughter
in the early afternoon.

Everything I loved
could be carried in the folds
of its dark pockets

where my hands clenched
their fistfuls of roses,

and everything I desired
bloomed there in the pretense
of letting go,

while scarlet petals rained down
and splashed to the floor
along the slick and splattered
length of its blackness.

Meanwhile, everything
I tried to hold onto
pricked shallow, thorny
furrows of resentment,

and everything I learned to accept
took root in the scars
and grew there in secret

along with the mundane seeds

of a throbbing, vestigial heart.

At some point I found out
that when the frozen nights
come early and unexpected

an old raincoat can save your life,
but it can just as easily serve
as your black and tattered funeral shroud,

or fall from you unnoticed,
never to be found.

I never knew finally
where I might have misplaced
that god-awful, stinking thing,

but those years took a war to end them.

# THE MANLY THING

## Margaret Karmazin

He was six feet tall, pale blond, beefy of build and dressed in Hell's Angels chic - leather vests, shirts with the sleeves ripped off. He wore thick, block-like rings on his fingers as if they were brass knuckles. When he was with the other men at the neighborhood bar, he drank hard and smoked a pack in one evening. His wife, Karen, was unaware of the full extent of his self-destructive habits.

"Really, Mike wasn't like this when I married him," he'd overheard her tell a friend. "Then he wore three piece suits and was an officer in the Young Republicans." That had been true, though during the day he worked for Spruce Trucking and now was garage manager.

He knew Karen liked men with a corporate look - to her, it was sexy and powerful. But he was nothing like that and while he knew it irritated her, he didn't feel it mattered. What mattered was that he looked and behaved like a man and taught his son to do the same. If he left the boy nothing else on this earth, that would do.

To personify his ideal, Mike spoke very little. He followed the example of Clint Eastwood characters, men of the condensed sentence, the monosyllabic answer. If someone should attempt to start a conversation such as, "Boy, that war is going on forever, isn't it? Wonder how long Congress will put up with it," Mike would grunt, "Good thing." (He was a devotee of Fox News.) If one of Karen's friends was stuck waiting for her to get ready, she might ask, "So what have you been up to lately, Mike?" And Mike would say, "Nothing worth noting," and that would be it. He'd snap open his newspaper.

Mike and Karen had a son. Brad was born with paler hair than Mike's and a Mensa IQ. Right off the bat, Mike trained him to think macho above all else. Only on Brad, it didn't fit quite right. If the boy had been born to other parents, the academic or progressive sort, he would have developed quite differently. He might have learned to fend off predators with a quick sense of humor or risen to tops in his class so that his acquaintances would have been intellectual and respected him for his clever and knowledgeable conversation. As it was, his brains went to waste while he put himself through the wringer to please Mike, ending up as a clumsy little freckled kid trying to look dangerous. Other kids couldn't resist kicking his ass, which only reinforced Mike's belief, that THEY ARE OUT TO GET YOU, so you'd better be tough. And Brad, worshipping his dad, obediently believed the same.

Brad also believed his father was invincible. "I got relatives who lived to a hundred," Mike bragged. Karen would elaborate, "His mother's eighty, but her mother and her mother's sister lived to over a hundred." Mike figured he'd inherited their genes.

"I'll show you how to use a crowbar," he told Brad when the kid was twelve. This didn't take much demonstration. "Try to hit them anywhere but the head," he said. "Do the head and you'll end up in prison for manslaughter. Or worse. If you can get the knees, you're set."

Though he tried not to, he remembered when he was twelve. Chubby, shy and reclusive, his body white and freckled, soft like bread dough. He'd hated himself. And those prick Bianchi brothers who tormented the shit out of him every chance they got. They'd be waiting, with or without their friends, always somewhere different so he couldn't count on anything, behind clumps of trees, up trees for that matter, inside open garages, behind parked cars, you name it, then jump out and grab him and twist his arms, shove dirt up his nose, punch him hard in the stomach, spit in his face. Soft little Michael Rhodes, reminded him what a useless pantywaist he was. He was humiliated on an almost daily basis. They gave him a break on Saturdays and Sundays if he stayed inside. He stayed inside.

It was some consolation when he shot up to six feet and the soft flub transformed into beef. He would have preferred hard, cut muscle, which he occasionally tried to obtain by basement weight lifting, but lost interest after a few weeks. Beefiness looked fine when you added tattoos and "sawed off" shirts. By his mid twenties, he could pass for slightly scary, which was enough to get by.

As Mike explained to Brad, "The skill is to walk a fine line. You wanna look mean enough that nobody wants to mess with you, but not so tough that they want to knock you down a peg. Get it?"

"Yeah," Brad had answered, but Mike never knew if he really understood, because he kept getting beaten up.

"I want him in the Catholic school," Karen finally demanded. "I don't care how much it costs."

Mike gave in. Why put the kid through hell? Today it was worse than Bianchi brothers. This was New Jersey. You had blacks and Hispanics and everybody else out to kill you any chance they got.

---

So that's where Brad had gone, where he could arrive in one piece, and finally graduated with decent grades. There was talk about his going to regular college, but Mike persuaded him not to. Waste of good money. Instead, he could put in some time at the local community college until he was old enough to join the police force. "I have connections," Mike told him. "You won't have trouble getting in."

Brad pumped iron in the basement and got "big". He shaved his head and wore a couple of earrings. He grew over six feet tall and his shoulders widened. Though Mike wasn't real happy about the earrings, he had to admit that Brad looked tough enough. Somebody might think twice before they harassed him now.

Mike was shaving when he noticed a swelling on the side of his neck. He went stone cold. It took him a few moments to work up the nerve to feel it. The bump was hard and irregular. How did he miss this before?

His heard pounded while his chest felt hollow. He leaned forward to look into the mirror, into his eyes. He felt a certainty that this was going to be bad. He leaned back and looked out the small bathroom window. Cars were going by; a dog was chained in the neighbor's yard. Life was going on as usual for all of them, but for him, everything stopped.

Eventually, he took in a breath and, heart still thudding, reached back up to reexamine the lump.

For weeks, going on months, he kept it to himself. He had to digest it. Somehow he'd always known, all those years spent breathing truck exhaust, he had known that it would lead to this. But though he had known, it came as a betrayal. A man does his job, takes care of his family, doesn't run around on his wife, keeps everyone comfortable and this is what he gets?

"We're going on a vacation," he told Karen.

"Why?" she asked, though she looked happy. "I mean, it's a weird time, September. You didn't want to go anywhere this summer."

"I'm just in the mood, that's all," he said firmly. "Let's go to Maine."

He knew she loved Maine, the rocky coast, lobster dinners, the sounds and smells of the sea. "We'll leave on Sunday," he told her. "Be packed."

They took their time driving up. He made a point of being nice, complimented her on her hair, held her hand once in the car. Though he didn't make much conversation, he did, in every way he could, make the trip perfect for her. It might be the last one they would ever take.

She seemed to notice nothing out of place, didn't turn suspicious. He supposed he liked that about her, that she was naive and trusting. He kept holding off going to the doctor and the thing kept growing. Finally, (how could she miss it?) Karen asked in an alarmed voice, "Mike, what is that?"

"It's shit," he said. "It's not good."

"Why don't you go to the doctor?" she asked, clearly alarmed.

It was an obvious question. The thing was really growing now, starting to deform his neck. He kept his voice hard. "I always knew I was going to die of cancer from that fucking exhaust."

She started to cry. "Well, go to the doctor!"

"Don't tell me what to do," he barked. "When I'm ready, I will." He saw her face close down, but he had to make things clear. If he was dying, he didn't want her fawning on him. It was enough to stand the one thing.

"I'm going to be straight with you," said the throat doctor a week later. Not a good sign when the family doctor got you in to see a specialist the next day. "I'm ninety-nine percent sure it's malignant."

He scribbled something on a notepad and picked up the phone. "Sherry," he said, "get an appointment for Mr. Rhodes here with Janson. He's with Wayne Memorial. STAT."

He turned to Mike. "It would have been better if you'd come in sooner. Why did you wait?"

Mike didn't answer. He wasn't really sure why he'd done it.

He had a leaden feeling of doom that pressed on him by the second. Sleep was nearly impossible. If he did manage to drift off, it was hot-wired and frightful and would end with a sudden jerk. He'd find himself with eyes wide open and heart skipping in a fast, exhausting beat as if he had swallowed a load of speed. In the dim light from the window, he could see Karen lying on her side, her back to him. Was she really asleep? Was she terrified? Most likely, she was going to be a widow. And that was weird because he was younger than she and he had the relatives who lived long, while hers died young. He had always assumed that he would be the one to see her out.

It seemed that everyone else was vibrantly alive and taking it for granted, like someone throwing away food unaware that another person would scramble across the floor for a crumb. Everyone around him had no idea how alive they were. Now Mike saw death, smelled its rot, shuddered in terror to imagine himself laid stiffly in his coffin and lowered into the dark, damp earth.

"Are you awake?" he whispered into the dark, but there was no answer. He could have sworn, by her breathing, that she was awake.

At first, he told his family he was not going to do anything. What was the point? He'd seen and heard about people they made suffer horribly only to die anyway. But the doctor was blunt. "If you don't do anything, you'll be dead in six months, and it won't be fun."

Did he really want the tumor to keep growing until it filled up his throat and choked him to death? Was that how he wanted to go?

The course of treatment would be grueling. The doctors were adamant about doing what Mike considered enough to kill a buffalo. But if that's what the bastards insisted upon, he would do it. Two operations, the chemo, and radiation too.

"We want to put in a stomach tube before we start the radiation," they told him. "Otherwise, you won't be able to get food down. Your throat will swell and be very sore."

"Never mind," Mike said. "If I say I'll get the food down, I will."

He could tell they thought he was an idiot, but he didn't care.

"Listen, Mr. Rhodes, this has nothing to do with your masculinity. If you think ahead, you'll want your nourishment. Good nourishment is important when you have cancer. Once we begin the treatment, your immune system will be compromised and there is danger of infection. The time to put the tube in is before beginning the treatment."

"No," Mike said. They were not going to put a hole in his stomach on top of everything else. "Believe me, I'll get the food down."

He watched them sigh and give each other what they thought were discreet looks. He didn't care.

"You might regret your decision, Mr. Rhodes," one of them said.

All the way home, Karen nagged at him. "Why are you doing this? If they tell you the best thing is to get the stomach tube, they know what they're talking about! What's the matter with you?"

"I don't want to talk about it," he said. "Drop it."

Sometimes he himself didn't know why he acted like this. It just felt it was important to do things his way. And why should he listen to doctors? They were money grubbing idiots, most of them. He could rattle off stories about people who'd almost been killed by them. A hundred years from now, they'd look back and laugh at what doctors did today, at what butchers they were. Doctors kept changing the rules and forgot all about what they'd claimed was the God's honest truth just five years before! Everyone in his family knew they'd killed his uncle Bill, gave him some medicine that damaged his heart. A friend of Karen's - they almost killed her too with some drug that made her stop making white blood cells. Doctor's were quacks. Why should he listen to them?

On the other hand, there was no denying he had cancer and that at the rate it was growing, he was beginning to resemble the Elephant Man. He could not believe this was happening. Was it real? Or had he fallen asleep and was stuck in some nightmare he couldn't wake from?

"Don't fawn over me," he snapped at his wife, as they strapped him into the gurney to wheel him to the OR. He saw her face shut down, saw her lip tremble, but he didn't have the energy to deal. The shot they gave him was taking effect and he was caring less and less about anything.

"I love you, Mike," Karen said.

Things quickly went from terrible to worse. They had to mutilate him to get the tumors out, even removing nerves and transferring one from his leg to his shoulder. One shoulder blade was now out of place and he could not get his left arm up on the table without lifting it with his right. The side of his face was deformed. He had prided himself on being a good looking man, but not now. There was no way anyone would call him that now.

He had a couple of weeks to "heal" before the radiation and chemo began. "I never heard of doing that at the same time," he told the doctor.

"Well, it's not common," the skinny little twerp said, "but in your case, we're bringing out all the guns."

"We're going shopping for a living room set," Mike told Karen after the operations. "Why?" she asked. "What's wrong with the stuff we have?"

"I want new," he said firmly.

She mumbled something, but he didn't ask her to repeat it. "You wanna come with me or not?" he barked. Apparently, she did.

He fixed the place up like he'd always wanted - big black leather sofa and love seat, flat screen TV, steel end tables. Got rid of all that fluff. He didn't care what Karen thought about it - she was going to be alive for a long time. She could change it after.

He felt inordinately angry at Karen, at everyone. She didn't know it, but several times during the day, he would get so worked up he wanted to punch her. Smug, healthy little thing, being solicitous and clingy. She accompanied him to most everything, the radiation sessions, the chemo. She was his wife, that's what wives do. Was she his friend? He didn't know. He didn't know if he had any friends. Speaking of which, he refused to go to the bar. To have them all pity him, whisper behind his back about how bad he looked? No, he couldn't take that, wouldn't take that.

Chemo started off all right, but evolved into pure hell. His throat felt like burned flesh, but by God, he got that food down! It took him a long time, maybe two hours to chew it to a pulp, then carefully swallow. Eventually, as the weeks wore on, he took to grinding it up in the blender until it was a gray-brown soup, then labored to down a half teaspoon at a time. Hours sitting in the kitchen forcing it. No flavor, no texture, no sensation except raw, hot pain.

When Brad was around, Mike was careful to let nothing show - not a wince or groan, no hesitation when moving about. He saved every bit of what little energy he possessed to cover himself.

"How you feeling, Dad?" the boy would ask politely and Mike would say, "Fine, son. I'm doing fine."

"But how's the chemo and stuff going?"

"It's going fine. I'm doing what I gotta do to take care of this. That's just what you do."

Stoic, tough, what a man's gotta do. He pulled it off, or so he imagined. Once he caught Karen shooting him a cynical look, but she said nothing. Did they discuss him behind his back? She probably talked to her friends and sisters, or God forbid, Brad. The thought of anyone feeling sorry for him made him cringe.

He told Karen, "I only did this for you and Brad. If it were just me, I'd have skipped it all and waited for the end."

But was that true? The thing was, when you were standing on the edge of the abyss, you did things you hadn't expected. Some of the time, he did believe that he endured these tortures for his family, but other times a small voice inside his head told him otherwise. He dismissed that voice because if it were telling the truth, wouldn't that mean he was a coward? He had not, in his life, been really tested, not having had to go to war or do anything dangerously physical. Was simply surviving a terrible illness a courageous deed? Women did that, even old ones. No, manliness called for more than that, didn't it?

He finished the chemo. Now though the soreness of his throat was lessening, he could not taste his food. "I'm a ruined man," he told his wife. "Look at this useless arm too."

"That's ridiculous," she said. "The measure of a man is not whether he can taste or if his arm works."

"Is it whether his penis works then?" he snapped. "I don't think that's working either."

"That also doesn't make a man," she said.

"Then what does, in your scholarly opinion?"

She didn't answer, but gave him a look he could not interpret. They were not a couple who discussed much. Or maybe it was that he didn't discuss matters. He didn't usually see the point. But now, sometimes, he wondered. He wondered what other men thought about. Maybe even women too.

It would hit him again that he'd had cancer, a very bad cancer. And nobody would understand what it felt like to have tried so hard all of his life to behave how a man should behave and now to find himself physically unable to do so. But what was he saying? How many men had fought in wars only to be disabled, deformed and worse?

At least he had not let Brad see him falter. At least, through it all, he had held up in front of his son.

One afternoon, however, he received a kick in the gut. He had thought he'd hung up the phone when Karen got a call. He figured he must have pressed the reset button instead of hanging up. A while later when he saw the phone lying there with the little red light on, he put it to his ear to see if anyone was still using it, and heard Karen say, "I don't know why he's got this macho thing all the time. It makes him look ridiculous. The thing is, we're all gonna die and if we're lucky, get old before we do and the longer you go, the more all that silly stuff melts away. Sometimes he just embarrasses me with that shit, but I'm hardly going to say so. You don't kick a man when he's down."

He was shocked. So that's how she saw him? After all he had been through, she was saying that? He pressed the off button hard and hoped she knew he'd been listening, the bitch. He had a sudden almost overwhelming urge to weep. If women only knew what men had to do, how they had to stiffen up in every imaginable way, to hold everything up. Everything up, so women like her could relax and laugh at him after being deformed, being made weak and ugly, after having been basically castrated!

Mike felt a lump push up in his throat, bigger and harder than the cancer had ever been. Not since he'd been a child had he felt such a thing. Knowing it was about to erupt, he darted to the basement door. His feet hit the stairs and as he rushed down, a terrible sob burst from him. It was followed by more, a continuous explosion, so that when he made it to the bottom, he had to sink onto the last step and curl up as if he were a child, his whole body shuddering uncontrollably.

He did not know how long he cried. His ass felt bone cold against the step. For a while, he was not sure he could catch his breath, but eventually, he managed. It occurred to him to fear that he might have torn something inside of his throat, though by now all the incisions had closed and the stitches dissolved. He checked to see if he was all there, as if he'd just survived a cataclysm.

He felt a stillness unlike anything he had known before and realized that he was lighter. As if he had released something dark and hard, something of cold metal that had lived inside of him for eons. He stood up and looked around gingerly.

When he was halfway up the stairs, he wondered if anyone had heard him. Did he care? He realized that he did not. It was a relief not to care. Was this how women felt? If so, it was good.

Brad was in the brightly lit kitchen when Mike reached the top of the stairs.

"Dad, you were in the basement? What were you doing?"

"How long have you been in here?" Mike asked instead of answering. He wondered idly if his eyes looked funny from the crying.

"I just got home, why?" said Brad. "Dad? Are you okay?"

So he'd noticed, thought Mike. Mike was silent a moment, then said, "That's a good question. Do you want me to answer it honestly? For a change?"

Brad looked startled. "Uh, yeah, I guess so."

"Physically, I don't know how I am. Is all the cancer gone? Who knows? Will I be dead this time next year? Who knows? They made a mess of me, although I guess they did the best they could, but I look like hell and my arm is useless. Mentally though, I'm pretty good all of a sudden. You know what I just did?"

Brad shook his head, his eyes wide open. Mike knew the kid had never heard his father talk like this.

"I bawled my eyes out. I sat in the basement and sobbed up my guts. And you know what? It felt damn good. Take my advice. If you ever feel like you'd like to blow your brains out, forget about being manly. Just cry like a girl. It clears up the air."

"If you say so, Dad," said Brad, looking slightly wary. "You want something to eat?"

Mike thought about it. "Yeah, yeah, I do. I want some ice cream. A huge bowl of it. Can't taste it much, but it's cold and it feels good going down."

"You got it, Dad," said Brad, opening the freezer.

Mike sat down at the table, lifted his bad arm onto it, and smiled.

# BLOODY 98

## Katherine Conner

Ida told her father not to build his store off Bloody 98, so when the roof caved in and knocked him stupid, Ida said to his loose, blank face, "Now, look at you, look what you done."

Ten years ago now, it was, and not once has his expression changed. He is there in the corner of the store, always the same, his mouth agape, the line of drool, like a sliver of sunlight, shimmering from his bottom lip and his eyes filmy as the morning mist that hovers over the highway. He is there, where she keeps him, his right wrist tied with cord to the heavy rocking chair that he built himself. But today she will sell that rocking chair and everything else and she will sell him too.

"All this time, I been here," she tells a man with a flat, squashed face who stands at the counter. She points to the highway beyond the open door. "I been here since they laid it down."

The man pushes a tangle of fishing lures at her.

"Hey," she says, "where're you from?"

The man clenches his jaw, looks ready to spit. "Canton," he says.

"You ever been down this road before?" Ida leans over the counter as she says this, too quick, and smacks both hip bones against the ledge. She is a thin woman, and her hip bones pose a problem in the store, where shelves are frequent, as are jutting mantles and rough-edged table-tops. She'll crack a bone, if she's not careful. She is only thirty-five, but feels that her bones are fragile, hollow as a bird's. "Hey," Ida says. "You know what they call it?"

The man is not looking at her, but over at her father, rocking in his chair in the corner.

"Bloody ninety-eight," she says. So often she has warned them, the travelers that stop on their way down to the coast or to Mobile or to places beyond, far, far beyond to what Ida imagines as a brilliant, watery landscape. She saw, once, a Technicolor film down in Mobile—reds and blues and greens so bright they made her eyes sting and this, she is sure, is Florida, Georgia, Louisiana. Places so beautiful that people die to reach them. "I seen it happen," she tells the man. "I seen people die right in front of this store." Most of them in head-on collisions on the two-lane highway: glass gleaming as it flies up from the road, the screech of tires and the sulfurous smell of burnt rubber, the great thunder-crack

68

of metal against metal. Yes, she has been here, front and center. Lone witness to the deaths of teenagers in coupes with the tops down, of middle-aged men half-drunk by mid-morning, fishing poles jutting from their truck beds. And women too, often in hats and gloves that, later, Ida finds scattered among the weeds, washes, and puts out to sell. Women, yes, and many with their children, some of them babies too.

"I never had any babies," Ida says. "Not even one that died." She didn't plan to say it, but it's her last day after all, and why shouldn't she tell this man? Her sister had given birth to a baby that died. And she'd had her show of grief, her graveside wailing, while Ida herself stood back, stood peering over shoulders and wide-brimmed hats that blocked her view, crowded her out.

The man gives her a squint-eyed stare, heavy brows dropped low, and then taps the fishing lures with his finger. "I'm in a hurry, Miss." His hair is matted against his skull and Ida has the urge to comb it through her fingers. She stretches her hand across the counter, palm up. From the corner, her father begins to hum. Always the same three notes, over and over until Ida can't think for it playing in her mind.

The man drops the coins into her palm, careful—it seems—not to touch her, and before she can think of something else to say, something to keep him here, he is gone.

"Look what you done," she says to her father. She stands over him, hands on her hips—a posture she picked up from her mother—but her father does not look. He only blinks and drools onto his chin and she'll have to shave him, make him presentable, before the doctors come; his stubble has grown back—how fast it grows! While the rest of him, his jutting shoulder blades and bony face, his skinny legs, his white, hairless stomach, lay inert, dormant, down to the scab on his left knee that, for some reason, never goes away.

"Just look what you done," she says. But she has things herself to do, more than usual. She has her past to sell, and only half of it priced and put on display. She'll put the rest out, all the junk her family left behind. She'll get rid of it all, her father included, and then she will shut up the store and head on down the highway herself, as far as Mobile and then farther, until she leaves that flat, black stretch of road behind her, like her mother did when she died, like her sister did when she married and moved up to Memphis. Like them, Ida will never come back.

***

There will be, most likely, a lot of junk leftover, a lot that she doesn't sell. If only she'd known in advance that she'd be going, she could've planned. Put signs in the window, Going Out of Business, Everything Must Go! Beautiful, hand-painted signs in big scrawling letters—how often she has imagined them, and the joy she would feel in hanging them, neatly, against the glass. Last Chance! Only 1 Day Left! How she would have loved to stand on the front porch and call to the passers-by: "Stop now or stop never! Tomorrow, I'll be gone!"

But it was too sudden. Only yesterday afternoon the doctors came. They came, sputtering up the highway in a faded blue truck, a tail of exhaust curling out behind them. They were on their way back to Jackson, they said, and all of them wore damp shorts and boots that squished and tracked mud onto the floor—the mud is still there, proof that they had come. But they looked like all the other men with their stained tee shirts and big, calloused hands, and she hadn't given them much thought at first. She was busy—a group of teenage boys had just slunk up to the counter with bottles of beer and a carton of cigarettes— but then, "What's he got?" one of the men said, and when Ida looked up, they stood in a loose ring round her father's chair. There were three of them all together, and it was the littlest, a man no taller than Ida herself, who had spoken.

"What's he got?" he said.

"A knock in the head, a long time ago."

The man kneeled in front of the rocking chair, waved his hands in front of her father's face. "What you got, there?" he yelled, right in her father's ear. When her father did not respond, the man stood and circled the rocking chair, eyeing her father up and down. "Look at him, Cal, Tupper," he said to the other men. They talked it over then, their heads bent close together, voices dropped low. One of them poked her father in the ribs, and when another struck him in the knee with his fist, the teenagers at the counter drifted over to watch. The little one tugged at her father's hair and, "See how he don't respond? Could beat him to a mess, probably, and he'd just sit there." They went over and over him, touched his face and studied his clothes, his posture, the loose flesh of his arms, and when he began to hum, "What else does he do?" they asked.

"Nothing."

They offered to take him. They would take him, they said, to the institution in Jackson, where they worked. They'd study him there; they'd seen nothing like it. "Of course," said the little one, "we'll give you something for him." He glanced at the teenagers huddled round her father, then, "Tomorrow," he said. "We'll take him tomorrow, after you close up."

While he spoke, the other two men wandered through the store. They sifted through the barrels of ice, touched the pretty tea cups laid out on a table, held the silver spoons up to the windows so that they gleamed in the sun. They studied the brass and tin and ceramic and they studied Ida too. She could feel them looking, looking from across the store, and "Yes," she said. "Take him, take him," before they could change their minds.

***

Above the store is the room where Ida sleeps, the room that was once her father's—a "study" he called it though, as far as Ida can tell, he never studied anything. What he did do, she doesn't know, but it was up here that the beam, rotten and water-logged, fell from the ceiling and caught him at the base of his skull, and "I hope it was worth it," her mother said to the still, white figure beneath the hospital sheets. And even now, years later, Ida wonders what her mother had meant. At night, she wonders as she lies there, in the narrow twin bed beneath the broken beam, her father's senseless humming drifting up from the cot in the store below. She wonders what he did here, what there could ever be to do, and she stares up at the cross-hatched pattern of the beams, her arms trapped beneath the covers, her eyes wide open and daring it to come down, the whole damned roof.

Up here, too, are the things they left behind. She takes inventory now, as she moves through the room, careful not to smack her hips against the slick wood table tops, the pretty, curving chair legs. Pencil in her mouth and paper in hand, she takes note of her mother's pink sofa and the big oval mirror framed in brass, her sister's porcelain cats lounging on the window sill, the years and years worth of glass décor hung or propped against the walls, the silk replicas of wild flowers, iron wall sconces shaped like birds, and framed prints of her mother's of ladies, their limbs long and plump and draped over couches, throats bare and white. Ida likes these especially, likes the ease and freedom with which these woman lounge. But she won't take them with her. She has made that promise to herself, that she will take nothing with her when she leaves.

There are also, folded and tucked inside a drawer, the presents from her sister in Memphis. Silk blouses and stiff, muslin slips, scarves with fringe and fingerless gloves, and still in its box, a collar made of real ivory lace, the card tucked beneath it—so you'll look nice. These could fetch a good price, the collar especially, and she would've put them to sell if it weren't for the men who now and then came into her life, like drifters, highway men. Up to no good, every one, but they liked her in silk and satin. They liked her with her hair loose and her neck and arms rubbed all over in perfume. One especially had liked lace, had buried his face in her lace blouse and taken it with him, along with three pairs of lace gloves and a handful of money from the register, when he disappeared. They all disappeared and this too was her father's fault, his dazed and open eyes, his slack-jawed expression. "It's unappetizing," the last one told her. "And to be honest," he said, curling his lip, "you favor each other. Same weird-eyed look." When he was gone and her mother's brooch with him, Ida said to her father, "Look what you done. Just look at all that you done."

She fastens the collar round her neck, fine soft lace tickling her throat, and she realizes that she may have somewhere to wear it, after all. A dance hall, a fancy sidewalk café, museums and galleries and shops—oh, the shops there will be! Better than the ones in Mobile. Maybe better than in Memphis, though she has never been to Memphis and can't compare. But she is sure that if she goes far enough, she will find all of this and more, things she can't imagine, and for a moment her hands linger among the silk and lace. She strokes the satin, fingers the tiny pearl buttons, and then she sweeps all of it up in her arms and carries it downstairs.

*** 

It is past noon, and there's no time to organize, no time for price tags or tidy displays, so Ida dumps it all in a heap on the floor—clothes and hats, old costume jewelry, ivory buttons, her father's trophy lamp with three deer forelegs as its base, and everything else she can carry downstairs. By the time the next customer comes—a woman in a crisp straw hat and striped dress—Ida has made several piles, all in the empty space in the middle of the store.

"My word," the woman says.

"Going out of business," Ida says. "Everything must go." But it falls flat. It's not the way she imagined it would sound, like the trill of a piccolo or the chime of a bell. It sounds like everything else. It just sounds like her.

"How much?" the woman asks, holding up a slip.

"Two dollars," Ida says.

"My goodness!" The woman holds her head high on her long, thin neck. "Used, too."

Two small girls, both in pig tails and ribbons, push past Ida and run giggling past the candy and soda aisles, past the barrels of ice and the rows of old books. They run past the tables bearing the dolls that long ago her father had whittled from wood—so long ago, it was, her father out on the porch, bent over in his chair and raw, bright wood curling from the point of his knife—and they stop finally at her father himself, asleep in his chair.

"What's he done?" one of them, the biggest, says.

The woman drops the slip and steps quickly over to her children. "Come away from there," she says, taking them by the hands. "Come away from him."

"Look here," Ida says. She grabs a doll from the table, holds it out to them. "Five cents for this."

"It don't look right." The smaller girl screws up her mouth. She is right; the doll is crudely shaped, its arms and legs too small for its head and its face smooth and flat, a tiny knick for a nose, a slash for a mouth. Her father wasn't much good at whittling.

"But what's he done," says the bigger girl, "to tie him up like that?" She tugs at Ida's skirt.

"He's got himself in trouble." Ida glares down at the doll in her hand. She tosses it into a pile of embroidered linen at her feet. "I can't tell you how much trouble." Because he had a knack, after the accident, of putting himself in harm's way. Too many times Ida found him with a knife in his hand or a gun pointed to his chest or on the ledge of the upstairs window, ready to jump. Once, even, she dragged him by herself from the pond behind their old home, his heavy, wet body weighing her down, nearly killing her. Accidents, all of them, her mother told her, before she died. "He doesn't know what he's doing," her mother said. "You got to watch him, Ida." Her mouth puckered and small as a dried fruit, her eyes the flat black of the highway, like two bits of tar sunk into that sallow skin. "You promise me you'll always watch him." Her sister had promised too, and then had broken the promise when the man from Memphis came along and asked her to marry him. "Don't blame me, Ida," her sister had said. "It's what I'm meant to do."

And so Ida was meant to stay here, to stay behind and watch her father because no one else would. Not her sister, who escaped through marriage or her mother who escaped through death or the one uncle, her father's brother, up in Natchez who sent a card when he heard the news: Y'all take care down there, it said. And then, scribbled at the bottom: He always was getting into trouble. He would get into trouble still if Ida hadn't taken, finally, to tying him to his chair. And it's worth it too, the wide-eyed stares of the customers, the extra time it takes in the evening to soak his chafed wrists in salt water. It is worth even the throb behind her eyes, the ache in her chest as every night, to get his blood moving, she kneads his legs like dough.

"What's that fluff round your neck?" The child gazes up at Ida.

"Oh, what a pretty collar," the mother says.

Ida brings her fingers up, is startled by the soft lace circled round her throat. She'd forgotten the collar.

"But have you got it on wrong? I think it's meant to lay flat."

"No," Ida says. "This is how they wear it in Memphis."

"We're from Memphis."

Ida rips the collar from her throat and tosses it at her. It flutters up in the air and then the bigger girl snatches it. "Take that back, then," Ida says. "Take it back there with you." She scoops up a slip and throws that at the woman too. "Take it, take it," she says. She drapes a blouse over the girl's head, throws a scarf round the smaller one's shoulders.

"You put those back," their mother scolds them. But the girls spin and skip in Ida's sister's gifts. They dance in fingerless gloves and silk sashes and, with Ida egging them on, they twirl about in the too-long slips until they fall together in a heap among all that Memphis finery. But the mother takes none of it when they leave.

Ida follows them out to the porch, waving a white handkerchief over her head. As the mother shoos them into the car, "I bet he stole something," one of the girls says. "And that's why she's tied him up."

"He did!" Ida balls the handkerchief in her fist and shakes it at them, as they drive away. "A dirty thief, is what he is. A common robber and no better than all the others who took from me. All of them crooks, every damn one." She has run out into the gravel lot to say all this, and when their car disappears against the sun-white horizon, she throws the handkerchief with all her force at the highway. The wind carries it back and it is caught, when it lands, in the tall weeds at her feet.

\*\*\*

She doesn't know how long she has been here, at the edge of the highway. The sun strikes hard against her left cheek and her blouse is damp with sweat. Cars pass, too close, blaring their horns. A shrieking gang of girls squeezed into a tiny Plymouth with the top down tell her to have a nice day. They maybe mean it, even though they laugh, and "You better watch it!" Ida says.

One of them, a pale blonde with bare, glowing shoulders, blows her a kiss.

"Don't you worry," Ida says, though they're too far off now to hear. "I'll have a nice day."

It'd be nice enough, if she could stop gazing out over the highway like a fool. As she steps onto the porch, a truck roars into the gravel lot, behind her. Two men get out. An older man and what must be his son—a long-legged teenager in a bright blue shirt, a lot of brown hair hanging over his forehead.

"Excuse me, Ma'am." The older man stands with his hat in his hands, his greased, dark hair flattened against his scalp. A rough-neck, her sister would call him, and his boy too, with their worn boots, their ragged shirts and dirty skin, and Ida feels she would like to bathe them. Scrub the grime from the creases of their necks and elbows, wash the film of dirt from their hair. She'd like to rub them raw, the both of them, make them shining and pink with the flat scrub-brush that every week she uses on her father, as her mother did before her. Seven years her mother has been dead, and Ida's clearest memory of her is the broad hulk of her back bent over the tub, her big round arms all covered in suds, the minty scent of the soap, and her voice—deep and monotonous, like the drone of passing engines, soothing, crooning to the man who frowned up at her from the tub. Often, he would jump to his feet without warning, a tall wet stalk of a man, so thin that his skin hugged up to his hip bones, his ribs.

And when her mother fell ill, Ida knew that now it would be her turn. It was all she could think, as her mother lay dying in her bed. Her mother lay dying, and the smell—it was a stink like road-kill, squashed rabbit and coon, smashed armadillo, the splayed bodies that so often Ida has shoveled up from the stretch of highway in front of the store. And it was that smell, that stink coming off her mother, her own mother for God's sake, and all Ida could think was that now she would have to stay here; she would have to stay and take care of her father. She wouldn't have a choice.

"Excuse me, Ma'am," the man says. "What you selling in there?" His voice is very deep, and smooth as cream. Familiar, somehow. "I need a shirt for the boy. He goes out there like that, he'll scare off the deer." He jerks his head toward the boy and his bright shirt. "I tell him he's got to blend, but he don't never listen."

Like sweet cream, or honey, that voice, so slow and thick and even, and she is certain that she has heard it before. "Listen," Ida says, "don't I know you?"

The man's mouth twitches, just briefly, then, "Don't see how you could," he says. "We most always stay up in Picayune."

"Or Lucedale," the boy says.

"This is Lucedale," says Ida.

"Excuse my language, Honey," the man says, "but the boy don't know his ass from his head. Born that way."

The boy curls his hands into fists at his sides, then stalks off toward the edge of the highway.

"That's not safe," Ida says. "Hey," she says, "you know what they call that road?"

The man beats the brim of his hat against his thigh. "We just moved down here."

"Bloody ninety-eight," she says. "You better tell your boy to watch it."

The man glances over at his son. "He always was getting into trouble."

Natchez. The word pops into her head, an image: Natchez, scribbled in pencil on a thick white card, dark, straight letters. Natchez, a word, another place she has never been. One more place to imagine, to conjure up from hearsay, from nothing: cobble-stone streets, maybe. Wooden bridges. Tall, bright pillars and clean blonde women. Men like the only one she has ever known from Natchez, her uncle, tall and gaunt and mustached and the sudden image comes to her: this man, this man here in front of her, only many years younger, swinging her high up in his arms, chasing her round the porch—and how much bigger it was then, the doorways and the stairs, the tall porch railing—and Ida laughing and running and her father, before the accident, stern and dark, scowling behind the counter. This man, with her now, and she squints up at him, at his shaven face, his sunken cheeks, and how can she tell? It has been more than twenty years since she has seen him, but it could be this man, the same man, older, dirtier, up to no good.

76

*\*\**

Inside, Ida stands with her back against the door while the man and his boy browse the aisles. They've yet to notice her father, asleep in his chair in the corner.

"I've got plums," Ida says.

"That so?"

"Over there by the canned fruit." She points them in the direction of her father. "Three rows down."

"I don't care for plums," says the man. "Where are the shirts?"

"How about the boy? He'd like a plum, I think."

The boy comes shuffling out of the candy aisle and stands with his thumbs hooked round his belt loops. He jerks his chin up at his father, says, "I never had one."

"You ain't starting now." The man's voice ripples forth, deeper, somehow, inside the store and Ida twists her hands together to keep from reaching out and slapping his bony face. "Look here," he says to her. "All we want is a shirt. Brown or dark green. Maybe khaki. That's all we need and we ain't buying nothing else."

"But some of it's yours," Ida says. She throws her head back, turns slowly on her heel and walks, her head held as high as the woman's from Memphis, over to the tables by the front window.

"Ours?" says the boy, following.

"This here." She turns to the boy, a pocket knife—blade out—gleaming across her palm. "You sent this a while back." She reaches next for a silver hair pin. "And this too. For one of my birthdays."

The boy plucks the pin from her fingers and weighs it in his palm. "Real silver, I bet."

"Put it back." The man stands where they left him, crushing his hat in his hands.

"And this one," Ida says, "you sent to him." She taps her finger against a cracked leather case that sits, unzipped, at the back of the table. "You had it full of things for him." Things she didn't understand—tiny vials of some kind of liquid, dark green glass, a finely wrought pipe. Her father had pulled them out with shaking hands, had spanked Ida when he caught her hovering.

"Get over here, boy," the man says. But the boy is bent over the table, fingering first the leather case, then a box of cigars, and finally a bracelet made of human hair.

"That's my grandma." Ida points to the tiny daguerreotype set in brass at the clasp. "I never knew her. She had famous hair." She rubs the tightly woven strands between her finger and thumb. "Of course," she says, "she was your grandma too."

There's a crash, a splintering of wood striking wood and the tinkle of breaking glass. The table lies on its side, the boy sprawled beside it.

"Get up. Get up, boy!" The man, who has knocked the boy down with his fist, stoops over the fallen table, the broken trinkets and scattered cigars. He yanks the boy up by the collar of his shirt and pulls him toward the door.

"Go on!" Ida darts in front of them, and stands blocking the door. "What did you come here for? Go on and see him. Look." She points over the man's shoulder at her father in his corner. "Look! Look!"

The man does not look, but stands there, his boy panting beside him. He stands there, close enough for Ida to smell him—mildew, wood smoke—and, "I'm sorry," he says. "Something's wrong with you."

Her hands fly up, claw at his face. The boy ducks out of the way, and Ida throws the whole weight of her body at the man, pushing him back. He catches her wrists, pins her arms to her sides. "Whoa there," he says, as if calming a horse. "Whoa now."

His hands, rough and dry as stretched canvas, burn like rope against her skin. She stares up at him, at the bags beneath his eyes, the deep creases that cross his brow, then, "You come to make me feel bad?" she says. "They told you I'm getting rid of him? I don't care if they did!" Her voice rises, too high—a squeal like faulty brakes. "I don't care! I don't care!"

From behind them, the boy says: "She's got a man tied up back here."

The man answers without turning to look. "I seen him earlier."

"What's wrong with him?" The boy appears at the man's side, his eyes wide beneath the mess of hair over his forehead.

"Looks to me," the man says, turning Ida loose, "like nothing." He bends, picks his hat up off the floor and sets it on his head. His eyes, hollowed in shadow, peer at her from beneath the brim. "Looks like nothing's wrong with him at all."

\*\*\*

The sun is setting by the time Ida has finished tossing everything into the road. The broken table, the lamps, the porcelain and glass, dresses and hats and fishing line, tackle, canned meat—all scattered across the highway. Cars pass, swerving out of their lanes to miss the rolling cans of fruit, the stacks of wooden crates, the fluttering linens and silks. It's not all of it, but it's all she can manage and she sits, panting, the front of her blouse soaked in sweat. East is where this highway heads, but Ida faces west, sun in her eyes. She sits on the heavy wooden trunk that she has hauled out to the edge of the highway. It is hot, and she hikes her skirt up to bare her legs, fans herself with a straw hat. The crickets have come out early, and the locusts, a slow, steady hum, always the same. Beside her, her father hums as well and she wonders, for the first time, if it's the bugs he's imitating.

A station wagon comes lumbering down the highway and, without slowing, shatters her sister's entire collection of porcelain cats. A face presses up to the passenger window, the mouth open and yelling something she can't make out—something directed at her—and then is gone. Gone, but followed quickly by a bulbous, shining Plymouth, engine roaring, that brakes hard and skids atop a framed portrait of her mother. The frame cracks and pops beneath the tires, and Ida presses her hands to her mouth to keep from crying out, to keep from jumping into the road and plunging her hands among the broken glass and splintered wood. Because it's what she wanted, after all; it's why she wore herself out for the last three hours. So the cars could flatten it all like possums, and she'll rescue none of it, not even her father who, loose of his cords, stands over her, blinking into the sun.

By the time the faded blue truck appears, most everything has been smashed or knocked down or blown aside. The road is littered with debris; along the shoulder on either side cars have trenched the grass, and the orange-red dirt, spun-up by tires, spatters the road. The truck slows, rolls to a stop several feet away, and the men get out. Four of them this time, and they lope together up the highway. They kick aside the wreckage, stomp on the broken glass. They swear, loud enough for Ida to hear. The little one, out in front, stops a few yards away, folds his arms across his chest and leers at her.

She knots her hands together in her lap, and for a moment—a moment only—it's as if she's waiting for her father to do something. As if she expects him to move, to run, to slap her maybe, or grab a table leg and charge them, these men, so clearly up to no good. But he does nothing. He stands there, his arms limp at his sides, his head tilted back and his eyes slit against the sun. In his hand is a wooden doll, one that he whittled for her sister, for her. He holds it by its middle, head down. A price tag dangles from its neck: 5 cents. Ida gazes at its pale, wood face, the rough, unformed features, and she wonders why anyone would ever want it.

# CANASTA'S RUN

## Travis Mills

Cane was the noticeable man who worked for Felis. He stood under a banana tree, his hair the color of ash tucked under a soiled Panama hat. Lines ran deep and black in his battered white face. His eyes were always bloody.

He picked day-old chicken from his molars with the wrong end of a match and leaned back so that the pitiful banana leaves came between him and the sun. He hated banana trees. If there had been another kind of tree around, he'd have climbed up in it, but the shabby group of banana trees was the only shade around and he took it. He felt the heat of the sun and remembered the day he stepped off a boat onto a long dock and walked a golden beach and how much he loved the sun that day.

Abdul's truck wandered up the dusty road. Cane used the right end of the match to light the cigarette between his lips. He rubbed the match dead on the tree.

The truck pulled to a stop. Cane stood in the clearing dust. Through the windshield, he recognized the scarred face and the eye patch he knew too well. The other face he didn't know. It belonged to a boy, nothing more than nineteen years old, with a cap of blonde hair and white teeth.

Abdul got out and came around.

"Who's he," Cane asked.

"Ready for your last run?"

"Who's the boy?"

"He's going with you."

"The hell he is."

Abdul grinned. The brown tobacco water leaked through his teeth. "Canasta, when you're gone, who will make the runs," he said and spit.

Cane dropped his cigarette and rubbed the back of his neck. He remembered when the sun had burned him but blisters had come and gone and left a hard crusted patch of skin.

"Get your ride out of the back so I can drive," Cane said.

Abdul moved around the back of the truck. As he followed, Cane glanced up at the boy. He sat still, his eyes firm and pointed down, his mouth open somewhere in the limbo of expression.

Abdul let the back door down and pulled a wooden ramp to the ground. He disappeared into the shadows where Cane could only make out the outlines of boxes—his supply load. He heard the snarl of a mule's breath and Abdul reemerged from the darkness, holding it by the ear.

As the mule descended the ramp, Cane fought the urge to run his fingers along its coat—a battered shred of fur and scars from an ambush years before. It was the last time he would see the mule and its owner. He had watched them both grow old.

Abdul climbed onto the mule. "Are you really going to leave us, Canasta?"

"I've waited twenty years not to see your bloody ass anymore. There's nothing you could do to keep me here."

He removed his eye-patch and scratched the white hairs over his pale, dead eye. He grinned. "Where will you go?"

"I'll catch a boat on the coast."

"And from there?"

"What do I do with the boy after I make the drop," Cane interrupted.

"He'll make the drive back."

"He won't be ready."

"He will or he won't," Abdul said and kicked the mule to tell it he was ready. It let out the closest sound it could to a groan and shuffled its feet.

"Goodbye, Canasta. Try not to kill yourself on this last one."

"If I do, I still won't have to see your ugly face again."

Abdul put his eye-patch back in place, spat, and turned the mule back up the road where he'd come.

Cane did not wait around to watch him go. He pulled the ramp up and slid it into the back. He closed the door and moved around to the driver's side. He swung himself up and inside and slammed the door shut while he turned the keys in the ignition.

It wasn't till the truck was bumping along at a steady pace that he looked over at the boy. He held a kerosene lighter in his right hand. With one finger, he flipped it open and the other, he sparked it. He never kept it long enough to produce a flame. He flipped it open, sparked it, all over again.

Cane dug for the pack of cigarettes in his belt. He steadied the wheel with his knees and struck a match on the door. He lit the cigarette he put in his mouth and rubbed the match out in his hand. He threw the pack at the boy. It landed in his lap.

The boy did not touch it. After a while, he looked at Cane and said, "I don't smoke."

"Then put the fire away."

The boy flipped it open, sparked it till he got a solid flame. He tugged one of the cigarettes out of the pack and held the fire with both hands while he lit it. He pulled smoke into his mouth without letting it into his lungs. He blew the smoke out and it clouded the cab.

His hand reached for the window lever. He pulled and it wouldn't go.

"Jammed," Cane said.

The boy looked at him and pulled again. After the second time, he gave up. He wiped the layered sweat off with his sleeve.

"When we get higher up, it won't be so bad. Right now, it won't do any good," Cane said and turned the truck around a grove of mango trees. He gazed at the pass before him, just a snake of a road leading up many hills. They reminded him of the bumps on a woman's skin when she was frightened.

He pushed the pedal to the floor for the last stretch of flat ground. The sun was finally crawling down and would soon hide. For that he was grateful, but he thought of how many afternoons he had come this way. Somehow he did not feel better because it was the last time.

"What's your name?" the boy asked.

"Cane."

The boy put the cigarette out on the seat. He threw the butt on the floor.

"That's not what he called you," he said.

Cane felt the road pick up beneath him. The slope had begun.

"What did he call me?"

"I don't remember. It was something else."

Cane shifted the truck into a lower gear. The engine talked back to him. He patted the steering wheel. "Shh," he whispered. "My name's Cane. I don't have any other name."

The boy returned to silence. He sat still with no lighter or cigarette to keep him busy. Cane watched the hood of the truck, where the sun still baked everything it could touch. He looked for a place to pull over and after a few hundred yards he caught sight of a ledge where the ground flattened out. He pulled the truck to a stop and shut off the engine. It hissed and he scratched the tough skin of his face.

"What are you doing?"

"Cigarettes," Cane ordered. When the boy handed them over, he got out of the truck. By the ledge there was a tree, dwarfed from wind and rain. It hung halfway off the hill. Cane leaned on the trunk and started smoking.

After a moment, the boy followed him. He listened to the truck hiss. He put his hand on the hood. A sharp pain gripped his face and he crouched with his hand between his knees, shaking. He glared at Cane with a blood vessel on its way out of his forehead. "How'd you know?"

Cane didn't have to answer him, the same way he didn't have to touch the engine with his hand to know it needed a rest. He'd spent long enough with the truck on his runs that it was just as much a part of his body as his ears or his toes.

The boy's pain eased and he shuffled over to the tree. He rubbed his hand and measured the lines on Cane's face with his eyes.

"I remembered," the boy said.

"What did you remember, kid?"

"I remembered what it was the one-eyed bastard called you."

Cane lit another cigarette with the first one.

"Canasta."

Cane pulled smoke and blew. He looked up in the branches of the dwarfed tree. A few monkeys ran about. They had small bodies and long tails. They reminded him of squirrels.

"Isn't that right?"

"He did," Cane answered. He took the hat off his head, leaned back on the bent trunk and covered his face. "It's going to be a long night, kid."

He closed his eyes and started counting. He counted the times he'd come up the hills. He fell asleep sometime after he reached one hundred and fifty-two.

He woke to the sound of knocking. He lifted the Panama hat from his face and prepared for the light to blind his eyes, but there was barely any, only the last gray shine of a sun that had just gone away. He heard the knock again. It came from the branches above.

A stone shot against the wood, grazed the leaves and missed one of the monkeys by a hair. The arm that had thrown it belonged to the boy. He stood a few feet away. In his once burned hand he held several stones. He threw another one. It missed completely and sailed down the hillside.

Cane got on his feet and put a cigarette in his mouth. He decided not to light it.

He walked towards the truck with his back turned towards the boy. He heard the sound of the stone again, but this time there was a thud instead of a knock. Cane turned to see one of the monkeys, knocked silly from the blow, fall off its branch and tumble to the ground. The boy ran to the ledge. He turned around, his eyes marked surprise, and he smiled with split lips.

Cane climbed into the truck and started the engine. He eased on the pedal and the boy ran to catch up as he started back up the hill.

Cane turned the wheel hard to the left. The truck cut wide around the bend and he remembered how close he was to the steepest stretch of the first hill.

He rolled down his window and felt the night's breeze coming at him. The jungle no longer looked bright green and warm, but black and alive. He glanced at the boy. The stones he held in his hand had fallen to the floor. His head lay propped against the door. It bounced up and down with the beat of the truck but he remained asleep, the way only a young man could.

Cane felt the earth rise beneath him once again. He pulled hard and pushed the truck into its lowest gear. His foot planted the pedal to the floor. The engine roared. He felt all the weight of gravity push him back against the seat. He looked out the window and he could only see the moon clouded in the sky.

A crash came from the back. He spun his head and pulled the curtain open. He heard another box fall and crash against the back door.

His mouth opened to curse but the words stopped when he noticed the boy, wide awake, staring at him.

"What's wrong?" the boy asked.

"They didn't pack it right."

Cane turned back to the wheel. He held it steady and pushed on the pedal harder, though he knew it was already pushed as hard as it could.

"What are you going to do?"

"Nothing I can do," Cane said, "but get to the top of the hill."

The boy shuffled in his seat. He pulled the curtain back and stuck his head in the darkness. Another box crashed.

"I'll see if I can hold them down," he said.

"Stay put. It's dangerous," Cane yelled.

"Will we lose some of them," the boy asked.

"We might."

"I'm going back there."

"It won't do any good." The words left his mouth while the boy climbed through the curtain opening into the back. Cane kept his eyes to the moon and waited for the world to tip forward. He listened to the boy as he fumbled around in the darkness, doing more harm he was sure than good.

He felt the ground start to level out and the moon vanished over the roof. He gazed across the shining jungle. The truck breathed heavy. He kept his foot on the brake.

The boy climbed back into the cab. Drops of blood fell from his left eyebrow. He sat and dabbed the cut with his palm. He looked at the blood, curiously, and continued to hold his hand over it.

Cane laughed. It was an uncontrollable laugh that began in his stomach. He tried to keep it in but the laugh exploded.

The boy glared at him, not angry, but frightened. Cane finished and lit the cigarette that had dangled from his mouth for a while. He let the truck roll ahead. It began a slow descent but quickly picked up speed and the wind blew hard through the window. It put out his cigarette and knocked his hat off his head.

The truck raged down the hill, flying over the bumps. The boy watched Cane, his gray hair blown back, a wide grin on his face, his foot not even near the brake.

The road leveled out a little. Cane's foot hit the gas. The truck raged on. He used all his strength to hold the wheel steady. Up ahead, the road curved and shot straight up another hillside. Cane wrapped his arm around the wheel. He slowly spun it to his right. For a moment, everything seemed to be turning over on its side. The boy held tight to the door. The truck passed around the curve and sailed up the hillside. They were still racing almost to the top and they set into a steady pace.

The boy sighed. He let all the air out of him and then took it back in. He wiped his forehead. Cane found his hat and put it back on.

They reached the crest of the hill. Before them, the road disappeared under a canopy of deep jungle. Cane brought the truck along the winding turns, palming the wheel in a slow descent.

"How long have you known Felis?" The boy sat with his legs crossed. The moonlight bounced off his eyes.

"I don't know him at all," Cane answered.

"But you work for him?"

He nodded.

"How long has it been?"

"Since the war."

"You fought in the war? You're awful old."

Cane ignored the boy. He pushed his hat back on his head and re-lit his cigarette. This time, he tossed the match out the window and watched it die in the night. "I was nineteen," he said.

"The first war?"

Cane blew smoke. He said nothing.

"You've been driving this thing for more than twenty years," the boy continued.

Cane filled his lungs.

"You must've done something real dumb to piss him off."

He let it out through his nose. "I did," he said.

The boy fell silent.

"What did you do?" Cane asked.

The boy pulled on the window lever again. He pulled harder when he remembered it was jammed.

"I asked his daughter to dance."

Cane flicked his cigarette out the window. "Did she dance with you?"

"She did," the boy said, his voice low, his tongue tired.

Cane rolled the window up because the wind blew cold on his sweat. He shook off a chill. "Where you from, kid?"

"Ohio."

"What are you doing down here?"

"Vacation," he whispered, "with some the old boys from the service."

"Where are they?"

"When things got tough, they went home. Said they'd come back with some dough to get me out."

Cane pulled the truck around a long corner.

"Can't say I blame them," the boy said. After a while, he muttered, "Where are you from?"

"It doesn't matter anymore."

"Where are you going when you get out of here?"

"I don't know. I haven't thought about it."

"You've been driving this truck for thirty years waiting to get out and you haven't given a damn thought to it? I'd have dreamed up a thousand things."

Cane glanced at the boy. He'd stopped holding the cut. A line of dried blood ran down by his ear.

"I think I might go to London," Cane said. His mouth felt dry. He had no spit left.

"England?"

Cane nodded. "There's a woman there I knew during the war."

"You think she's still around? She's probably married by now."

"Maybe."

He licked his lips. His fingers fumbled through his pack of cigarettes and told him there was only one left. He threw the pack at the boy. The boy picked it up and took the last cigarette out.

"You ever going to tell me why he called you Canasta?"

"Sure."

"When?"

"When we get to the end of line."

He let the pack fall to the floor. He rolled the cigarette between his fingers.

"You going to smoke it or play with it all night long?"

"I'll save it for later," the boy said and put it in his shirt pocket.

The truck brushed against a tree. Cane straightened them out. There wasn't much road to see. He looked ahead in the hazy mist that drifted through the jungle.

"What does this girl in England look like," the boy asked.

"I doubt she's a girl anymore."

"Well what did she look like?"

Cane spotted something ahead. He pumped the brake. Through the mist, the headlights caught the outline of a large black mass.

He pushed hard on the breaks. The truck came to a stop, ten feet short of the thing in the road.

"Don't ask any questions," Cane hissed.

He leaned over the steering wheel and looked down past the hood into the road. After a moment, his right hand went under the seat. There was a snap. His hand reemerged with a Colt. 45. He checked to see if it was loaded. It was.

Quietly, he pulled the handle to the door. He stepped out. The air was wet. He hung close to the truck. The engine breathed on him as he made his way around it, finger on the trigger.

He bent down over the mass. His free hand reached out and wrapped around the water buffalo's one unbroken horn. He then felt the core of its body, closest to where he assumed its heart might be.

He heard a sound. The boy tip toed around the other of the side of the truck. He bent down next to Cane.

"Can we drive around it?" he said, softer than a whisper.

Cane took his hand away. He wiped it on his pants. "Yes, we can."

He stood up straight. He looked forward into the road. It disappeared in the darkness and the mist. He turned to his right and his left. Black green leaves held still in what looked like a wall of bushes and trees. There was only the sound of a parrot, far off.

"What's wrong?"

"Why did this thing have to die in the middle of the road?"

He heard a branch snap. He clung to the bumper.

"Lie down," he ordered the boy. The boy crouched down.

"Lie down next to the buffalo." The boy flattened himself to the ground. Cane looked under the truck. He began to crawl beneath it but stopped. Crouched, he moved slowly along the truck, back to the driver's side door.

A shot rang out. He felt the bullet zip past his ankle before he heard the sound. There was another that followed it but he was already suspended in the air, hanging off the side mirror. He was just as happy that the bullets had missed the tires as his feet. He briefly imagined the nightmare of being stranded without a way out of the hills.

He heard muffled shouting from the other side of the trucks. Seconds went by. Footsteps started on the road. He let his feet down and rushed around the back of the truck. He met a man dead on. It was only luck that he held his gun the way he did; it slid right up to the man's belly. He fired. He noticed the man's features after he put a second bullet in him. His mustache was wet with the blood he spit from his lips. He held his shaking gut with two fat hands until his gut stopped shaking and he stopped breathing.

There were no footsteps left to be heard. Cane scratched his chin with the Colt. He moved one foot at a time to the other side of the truck. He peaked around the corner.

The boy poked his head up from the dead buffalo. He spotted Cane and waved. Cane watched him hover over the carcass before he crawled away. When he reached the front wheel, he got to his knees and when he reached the passenger door he got to his feet. He slid along, coming towards the back of the truck.

A body moved from out of the bushes. The second man did not make a sound. He held a rifle by his side like it was his arm. He too watched the boy work inch by inch; he hadn't seen Cane yet.

Cane took aim at the man, the Colt at his hip. The man pulled the rifle to his shoulder and traced the boy's path.

Cane bit his tongue. He watched the boy and his blonde hair in the night and kept the words inside him. He waited until the shot rang out. He heard the whimper and then he knew. He fired and caught the shooter by surprised. The man fell on top of his rifle, face down.

Cane peaked around the side of the truck. The boy lay crumpled in a ball. There was a hole in the center of his back. Cane bent down to check if he was breathing. He wasn't.

He stuffed the Colt in his belt and pulled the boy up. He dragged him to the passenger door, leaned him against the truck, opened it up, and with some effort, hauled him up into the seat.

He went around to the driver's side and climbed in. He started the engine. The truck reversed and maneuvered around the buffalo. Cane drove on through the misty jungle road.

After a minute, he looked over at the boy. He leaned against the door, body bouncing along with the bumps in the road. Cane reached over and pulled the last cigarette from the boy's pocket. He struck a match and lit it. He pumped on the brakes and took a turn. He could see the next hill. Behind it and the next one, there was the end of his run. He blew smoke and looked at the boy again.

"It's better like this," he said.

He fell silent and remained so. He realized he was talking to himself.

# JOHN GREY

## Religious Experience At Joe's

It's a dark and quiet,
smoky page
from the book
of martyrs.
Soft strains of hymn
float out of the jukebox.
Bottles gleam behind the bar
like evening stars.
Faithful witness throats
guzzle brave beers,
celestial whiskeys.
Men walk on water
in the bathrooms.
With a little powder
on the cheeks,
red on the lips,
women change water
into wine.
Every drunken voice
delivers sermons.
Each besotted brain
rings bells.
Later, bars close,
streets empty,
apostles return home
to those of little faith.

# MICHAEL SHORB

## Body Count

The carnage was unimaginable.
Right where the second line
turned into a broad boulevard
lined with palm trees
bodies were stacked like cordwood,
still dressed in Chinese-made
Hawaiian sports shirts,
resembling
        viewed from a distance
a tangle of poisoned
tropical birds.

Making a point with the focus group,
the next stanza features
the barely cold body
of a shapely blond in a negligee.
Authorities standing around,
brief flashes of photographer's
light stun the air.

It's better not to even view
this next part, where a loner snapped,
bringing his guns to
the dance or the school or
the breaking of morning on the factory floor,
or search the dead eyes
of the small time dealer and pimp,
crumpled on his city corner,
or scan the slight possessions
of the one who just expired
in a room at the SRO,
late in the afternoon,
shadows casting
black patterns on a white wall.

# PURGATORY IS A ROCKING CHAIR

## Jim Ryals

Gabriella Glass stood up from gathering her morning harvest of strawberries, smiled as she looked at the lake, and died. She lay there crumpled on the ground, her khaki slacks and brown t-shirt making her body look more like one of the three compost piles than one of the newly departed. I sat there on the porch and rocked, chewed on the mouthpiece of an old pipe, and waited.

Fortunately, Miss Gabby, as people called her, had put her strawberry beds right up at the front of her yard. She said it was because the light was better for berries there, but in reality she liked to have the neighborhood children reaching their little hands through the pickets of her fence to feast on the fruit. "Better them than the darn crows," I'd overheard her say more than once. It was those same children who discovered her body; they screamed as loud as they could that Miss Gabby was hurt and ran back to their mommas.

Miss Gabby grew up here, married Baxter Fain Glass IV, the first person in our town to leave the state for college, Annapolis at that, and moved away just as soon as the wedding was over. But Miss Gabby moved back in 1966 after living for a time in Norfolk, Virginia, home port of the aircraft carrier USS Forrestal, the ship her husband was stationed on. Miss Gabby's first and only child, Gregory, had been born with all kinds of problems. Back then, we called him a mongoloid. These days' people would more correctly say he was diagnosed with Down's Syndrome. Whatever you want to call it, Lt. and Mrs. Glass decided that, since the Forrestal was about to deploy to Vietnam, it would be better for the mother and child to move back home where there would be friends and family to support the two of them. Lt. Glass' father found a small cottage two blocks up from the lake with a nice sized lot. Miss Gabby and Gregory moved in as soon as the papers were signed and the lawyers were paid.

Gregory was seven when they moved back. He lacked the mobility of most children; he wasn't crippled exactly, he just seemed content to sit himself in one place and watch the world go by. His weight might have been part of the problem; he was a bit beyond being called "big boned," moving more towards being called, though not to Miss Gabby's face of course, "fat as a pig." He'd sit in the yard, his pink legs looking themselves like a couple of piglets, watch the grass and, with almost methodical effort, pluck a piece of the nearest plant, and eat. And as if those plants were pure lard, Gregory continued to expand.

Now, likely because of his size, Gregory was not one to make any excess movements. In fact he was about as mobile as an alligator on a cold winter morning. But the sight of the mailman walking down the road in his grey shorts and pale blue shirt would, like nothing else, put Gregory in motion, running and heaving, wobbling and grinning, his normally doughy skin flushing with excitement, until he arrived at the mail box. The mailman, one of only three people to ever see Gregory smile, would grin back at the boy and hand Gregory his favorite thing in the whole wide world – a letter from his father. Most of the time, Lt. Baxter's letters would actually come in the form of reel-to-reel tapes. Gregory would run back into the house, tear open the envelope and thrust the roll of glossy brown tape at his mother. If she wasn't immediately compliant, he'd pull out the tape player and bang it on the breakfast table until he got what he wanted. After Miss Gabby had placed the reel onto the machine, he'd rush in to his room and bring out a photograph of Lt. Glass in a gold frame. Then he'd listen to his father's voice. Gregory's face would become at once effervescent yet still, as if the boy had entered a state of rapture. When the tape ended, he'd press the rewind button and listen to it all over again. Miss Gabby was a woman of infinite patience, as far as I'm concerned, though after the 9th or 10th replay, she'd insist on putting the machine and the tape away, telling the boy that he'd wear them out if he didn't stop.

It was about this same time that Miss Gabby drove to Baton Rouge and bought a television set. It was delivered with a little bit of fanfare since it was the first color television on the block. From the first episode of "The Lone Ranger" that Miss Gabby turned on to check that it was working, Gregory would never voluntarily be much more than a foot from that television. It got so bad that Miss Gabby took to unplugging it and locking the front door to the house to keep Gregory from lumbering back in and plopping himself down to watch another show.

Gabby planted the side yard, the yard closest to the lake, with vegetables and had a crew plant the back yard with Satsuma and pecan trees. She'd spent quite a bit on two of the trees as they were larger and more mature and towered above the others. Between these two, she strung a hammock and let Gregory loll on it in the afternoon, splayed on his back, watching the clouds meander across the turquoise sky. All the while, she worked her plots of vegetables and fruit, weeding and watering, pruning and staking, looking more like a sweaty field hand than the wife of a naval officer. Mother and son seemed quite content with their lives and each other.

Their self contained, easy going (at least for Gregory) routine endured even into the heavy heat of July, a heat made all the heavier by the cloying smell coming from the paper mill some fifteen miles away; a smell that made the entire town feel like it was trapped inside a child's paste jar. Gregory had his eighth birthday party on July 10 and Miss Gabby invited all of the children of the neighborhood. Gregory didn't seem to notice them much, though he did have a good time drawing on the front walkway with frosting from the cake.

Things might have continued in this happy way indefinitely except for a small electrical surge in an airplane on the USS Forrestal, half a world away off the coast of Vietnam. That surge caused a rocket to light off and hit the fuel pod of a nearby jet, a jet loaded with aviation gas and bombs. The result was the start of one of the worst naval disasters since World War II and killed 134 men, including one Lt. Baxter Fain Glass IV. Lt. Glass was running from his burning A-4 fighter jet when a bomb nearby, bathed in burning jet fuel, cooked off. The explosion was so intense that he and most everything on that section of flight deck simply disappeared into the Gulf of Tonkin. No body was ever recovered. At about 2:30 on an August 1st so hot that the sky seemed to be melting, two naval officers in sweat-stained uniforms marched past the strawberries and knocked on the door to give Miss Gabby and Gregory the news.

It was still that night, an eerie stillness that set my teeth on edge, so hot that the tree frogs were too fatigued to sing and the mosquitoes' hum seemed muted as if they were encased in molten candle-wax. The only sound was the drone of air conditioners for those lucky enough to have them. I sat down in a rocking chair on the porch across the street and stared at Miss Gabby's house. It didn't take long before I heard a strange keening sound, sort of like a cat that's been hit by a car. Sort of like the sound that Miss Maple's cat made upon seeing me in that rocking chair just before it arched its back and bounded into the night. The sound grew louder and deeper until it threatened to overwhelm even the hum of the air conditioners.

In a moment, there was the breaking of glass and a series of thuds from Miss Gabby's house. I heard the strangling pop of light bulbs, the clattering bang of shattered crockery, the hammering thuds of heavy furniture, thuds that shook the ground as they pounded at the darkness. Doc Tremblay arrived and ran inside. An ambulance followed soon after, its red lights wheeling around, bathing Miss Gabby's cottage in an evil, flickering redness, looking like what I had once thought purgatory would look like, those times I thought about purgatory, which hadn't been often until quite recently. Doc Tremblay appeared at the front door to Miss Gabby's house and he directed the ambulance driver and his assistant into the house. I chewed on my pipe and waited. I heard the words "sedated" and "use restraining straps" and then all three of them reappeared with someone strapped to the gurney. It was poor Gregory, looking more like a rotten, lichen covered log than a little boy, a boy moaning, despite the drugs, with unrestrained grief. It seemed to take forever to get Gregory into that ambulance, but at last they did and away they went with Doc Tremblay and Miss Gabby following in Doc's car.

A week later, Officer Bosco arrived with the mayor, who just happened to be Bosco's uncle, and a crew of prisoners, hard to miss in their identical black and white striped jump suits. It was this last group who began working on Miss Gabby's house. They poured pilings and then erected a frame around the existing structure. Despite the heat and despite the frequent thunder storms almost every afternoon, it seemed like those prisoners worked ten hours a day for three straight weeks. The prisoners were strangers, and when their jail time was up, they scattered, like dandelion seeds in a summer breeze, or, depending on your feelings towards the incarcerated, like cockroaches under a kitchen light, to parts unknown so no one ever got the opportunity to ask them about that construction.

In less than a month there was a new house where the little cottage had been. It was a huge thing that dwarfed the houses on either side, white clapboard more than two stories high and gabled at the top, with dark green shutters all around. Miss Gabby seemed satisfied even though it had eaten up a fair bit of her garden, and cast a couple of hours of shade on her tomatoes. Doc Tremblay and Officer Bosco were frequent visitors to the new house and they brought boxes and packages every time they arrived. Frankly, if I hadn't known Emily Tremblay, Doc's wife, so well, I might have suspected something going on between Doc and Miss Gabby, he was there so often with presents; but I knew better.

Well, the entire town came out for Lt. Glass' memorial service, all looking properly grim in their black suits and dresses, handkerchiefs dabbing foreheads as often as eyes in the sweltering church. It was a short service and Miss Gabby offended almost everyone by failing to have a wake. Not to be put off, the women of the town mixed and baked, simmered and stewed, and appeared that afternoon in twos and threes with casseroles and hams, pitchers of sweet tea and punch. Miss Gabby offended near the entire town a second time by refusing to let anyone inside her house. Everyone was curious as to the new addition, it had gone up as quickly as anyone had ever seen, and had been built with prison labor no less. But she refused, keeping everyone on the porch, dashing in and out to put food in the refrigerator or to bring dips and crackers out onto the porch, her black dress clinging to her slight frame like a wet shroud. People complained about her rudeness for nearly a week, but the town's a forgiving lot, especially to a young widow who had so recently also given up her child, and town's thoughts turned to other things or, more truthfully, to other people.

And, that would seem to be that. Oh, there were a few odd things from time to time; the gals at the pharmacy pointing out how many groceries Miss Gabby purchased, gossiping that she was feeding some back door lover, guessing that it was poor Hank, who dropped by from time to time to trim the trees. Then there was that period where she seemed to sleep all day and be up all night, couple of years actually. She tended her garden in the evening and then stayed up with her lights on far into the night. She returned to sewing and, from her open front windows; the sewing machine could be heard moaning that odd tortured sound, kind of like a frog that's been put to work, with the shuttle clacking an accompanying rhythm. Oddest of all was the electronics she bought. She was the first person to buy a VCR and, later a DVD player. Yep, Miss Gabby was addicted to the boob tube. Or so it seemed.

As to poor Gregory, no one talked much about him after conversation about that violent evening died down. He didn't attend his father's memorial service, of course; no one expected him to. Afterwards, Miss Gabby never volunteered any information about him. If asked, she'd sigh and say that he was in a good place and, no, it didn't look like he would ever leave. After awhile the town stopped inquiring about him at all.

Time passed and folks all got older and maybe a little more set in their ways. Well, some did, others not so much. The Chief retired in 2006 and made a failed bid for the congressional seat. After that, he played golf, his golf cart was probably the only one in the state with a built in police scanner, and talked LSU football. Doc never actually retired, he just stopped taking new patients and slowed down as the old ones moved away or passed on. The two men played golf together a couple of times a week. I just continued sitting on the porch, rocking and waiting. And then one day Miss Gabby died.

***

The first official person to arrive was Officer Pete Singer. He parked his car in the middle of the street and listened to Missy Alexander, who had flagged him down. Officer Pete also listened to assorted children explain the situation with much pointing at Miss Gabby's body and a general waiving of hands, shuffling of feet, picking of noses.

Having heard enough from Missy and the children to get some idea of what had happened, Pete called the station for an ambulance. Miss Gabby was there among the strawberries, wicker basket by her side, and the morning's pick of fruit, set free of their confinement, strewn through the picket fence and across the sidewalk. Officer Pete jotted a few things in a little notebook and walked over to where Miss Gabby lay. He checked her neck for a pulse and then took a long look at the body without moving it, stood up, and shook his head at Missy, confirming the obvious. He instructed her to move the kids off the sidewalk since they'd started eating Miss Gabby's dropped strawberries, the fruit being potential evidence and all, and stepped towards his patrol car. A noise, muffled as if buried under Miss Gabby, caused Officer Pete to jump and pivot back towards the body. He rolled the corpse over and retrieved from her waist a baby monitor.

The monitor was playing the sound, I could hear it plain as day, of a television show and then a voice cried out, "Momma, hungry." It was a deep voice, sonorous almost, but the formation of the words was lisping, fumblingly pronounced like those of a child or even a baby just learning to talk.

Pete asked if anyone else lived in the house. The children answered "no" in a dysfunctional chorus. Missy started to shake her head, frowned and stared down at Miss Gabby. After a long pause she stated that, as far as she was aware, Miss Gabby lived alone.

Pete looked up at Miss Gabby's house, resting his hands on his hip, the fingers of his right hand picking at the leather safety strap of his holster. After a moment's pause he walked up the stairs to the porch and peered into the house. Slowly, as if expecting trouble, he opened up the aluminum screen door, weathered and white spotted with age, and walked inside. Unseen, I got up from my rocking chair, stretched and yawned, more out of habit rather than need, and tagged along, since I had been curious about the house myself for years.

Officer Pete stepped inside, the steps from his heavy work shoes echoing as he did so. His eyes adjusted to the gloom and he made out a work table festooned with sewing patterns, thin brown sheets of paper fluttering like startled birds in the slight breeze. Next to the window was an old Singer sewing machine with two immense pieces of off-white canvas fabric hanging limply on both sides of the needle, one half neatly stitched and the other awaiting its fate. He walked over and picked up a copy, one of several, of Esphyr Slobodkin's book "Caps for Sale," on an adjacent table. Also on that table, looking like ticker tape before it is thrown out a window at a passing parade, were strips of paper. Officer Pete picked up one. It was taped together from sliced notebook paper and numbered, in what appeared to be a woman's script, from 1 to 108 with 108 at the bottom.

It was at that moment that Pete's focus shifted from the small, odd items set on tables, organized like work stations, as if in an office or a factory, and focused on the large. He looked up and saw that the entire edifice was a single large, cavernous actually, room. In the center of that room, a room devoid of any signs of domesticity, a room containing only those items strictly necessary to further the purpose of the former owner, though only hinting at what that purpose might be, sat the original cottage that Miss Gabby and Gregory had moved into in 1966. He opened a cabinet situated next to the white clapboards of one side of the house and found that it contained a multi disc dvd player, turned on and playing. Wires exited the cabinet, travelled a couple of feet and then disappeared into a PVC pipe that stuck out from the side of the cottage.

Outside, a car came careening down the street and slammed to a halt behind Officer Pete's patrol car. From it Chief Bosco and Doc Tremblay emerged. They were dressed in shorts and polo shirts, and it was pretty clear that they had come from the golf course, given that Doc Tremblay still had a club in his hands. They bounded out of the car, ran to Miss Gabby's house and up the stairs, their combined weight causing the treads to moan in protest. Chief Bosco threw open the door with such force that Officer Pete whirled and drew his weapon.

"Chief, you know better than to charge an officer like that," Officer Pete chided. He took a step backwards and stared at the men, at their skinny, veiny legs, in Bosco's case, legs that seemed too skinny to support his enormous belly, at their skinny arms, at their faces, grim with determination and sagging with age. "Doctor Tremblay, put down the club, please. Chief, hand me your weapon."

Each of the men stared back at Officer Pete, at the grey uniform with the black stripe on the side of the pants, at the black leather utility belt, slung low over his narrow hips and exercise-tightened stomach, at the swell of his chest, a chest used to constant weight lifting and magnified by his bullet proof vest.

Doc Tremblay looked at the 5 wood in his hand as if seeing it for the first time. Then he leaned it against a table. Chief Bosco pulled his revolver out of its holster at the small of his back with two fingers and handed it to Officer Pete who took it, emptied it of cartridges and handed it back to the Chief. He pointed at the windowed side door of Miss Gabby's original cottage, the view through the glass occluded by heavy shades. "Would one of you open it, please?"

"Pete, hear us out first," suggested Doc Tremblay, "what you're going to see inside may seem a little strange."

Officer Pete looked around the huge room, at the various work stations, at the cabinet containing the DVD and then at the cottage before turning his gaze back to Doc Tremblay. "This all looks a little strange to me, Doctor. Now, Chief, open the door."

The two men glanced at one another and hesitated; each seemed unwilling or unable to perform the act demanded. Officer Pete glanced down at the floor and then, returned his gaze at the two men, "Gentlemen, open this door or wait for the locksmith on the porch and in handcuffs."

With a final glance at Bosco, Doc Tremblay fished keys from his pocket and twisted one into the lock of the side door to the cottage. He gently pushed the door open and we stepped into a small kitchen. The counter's Formica top gleamed turquoise blue in the fluorescent lights and a white refrigerator, its rounded corners and chrome latch and hinges bearing testament to its age, hummed softly. Above the sink was a window, its blind drawn and its curtains, displaying pieces of fruit drawn in reds and blues and greens, closed, yet through which light peeked through in places, flickering like distant stars or dust motes at sunset. In the sink were dirty breakfast dishes and a cast iron frying pan, waiting to be cleaned.

Officer Pete glanced at each of the men, his face a mask of confusion, then started down the hall, towards the sound of a television. I followed him into the first room and found a queen sized bed, made, covered with a white knit spread. A low wooden dresser stood next to it, intricately carved with figures from an Asian pastoral scene. On top of the dresser a silver tray, on which lay a bone-handled brush and sundry bottles and tubes, was reflected by the large mirror that sat on top of the dresser. A framed picture sat on the matching carved-wood night stand, a picture of a man and a woman, she in a flowing wedding dress, her arm holding his, he in a white uniform, smiling and holding a pipe in his free hand.

Before Pete could stop him, Doc Tremblay walked down the hallway, stepped around an aqua colored canister vacuum, and opened a door. "Hello, Greggy!"

It was like looking at pictures from an old Life Magazine article about decorating for your son, like being transported back in time, as if time itself had stopped in the 1960s. The bed was neatly made with a beige ripcord cover, over which half a dozen G.I. Joes were seated in various stages of undress next to a stuffed Winnie the Pooh, equally nude, lacking one eye, white stuffing emerging from one arm, looking like the underarm hair of an old man. Over the bed headboard was a carved wooden crucifix that had been shattered at one point and repaired; there were lines of dried glue glittering in the light in several places, and the feet of the Christ figure were missing. On the wall beside his bed was a strip of paper identical to those in the living room, vertically numbered, but this one's numbers only went from 1 to 107.

At first glance, this room could have been any young boy's bedroom. But closer inspection revealed that the old television, too large for the room, didn't quite cover the hole where the television's original picture tube had been removed. The bed in the room, at second glance, was held off the ground by heavy wooden posts and the rails, painted white like the headboard and holding the mattress in place, were made from 2 x 4s. Similarly, the rocking chair, with its back pointed at the door, white like the rest of the furniture and crowned with a carved cowboy hat on the upper back rail, was larger than child sized. It was larger than adult sized and the thick braces across the back made the chair seem more fitting for the repose of something large and simian, rather than small and human.

In that chair, with his back to the door, sat the room's inhabitant, who, appearing at first glance to be in fact large and simian, was dressed in white canvas dungarees, dungarees that seemed hard pressed to hold in the flesh that had been stuffed into them and which oozed over the sides of the chair. A light blue yoke shirt with white pearl buttons--buttons that threatened to pop open at any moment from the strain, between which slabs of grey flesh protruded--attempted to cover his torso. Bisecting shirt and pants was a leather gun belt and holster, mostly hidden under rolls of flesh, the latter holding a small revolver with a white plastic handle. On his head was a white cowboy hat that shielded his face until he looked away from the television set and towards the four men. The face was that of a bloated corpse, drowned days earlier but missed by the scavenging crabs, or buried and forgotten for weeks before being dug up, with eyes that were so covered by rolls of fat that even the epicanthic folds, that hallmark of Downs syndrome, were lost. His hair, of which only small portions peeked out from under the hat, was the salt and pepper colors of middle age. He scratched one of the folds of his belly, twisted his head and frowned as he looked at the men. Then he slurred at Doc Tremblay, "More pills?"

Doc Tremblay smiled at the figure, "Did you get your pills this morning, Greggy?"

The figure smiled and nodded, his jowls and the folds of his neck jiggling in time. Then he pointed at the television. "Roy Rogers."

"You go ahead and watch it, young man." Tremblay reached over and patted the doughy figure on the shoulder.

Gregory Glass stared up at Officer Pete who was taking in the room. Pete's mouth was set in a thin line and his eyes glittering with anger, gun out of its holster and still in his hand. He stared hard at the strip of paper taped to the wall. He stared for so long that Gregory looked back at what he was staring at and saw the strip of paper. Then he looked back at Officer Pete, collected his thoughts for a second and said, "Hundred seven days." A pause. "Daddy's home." Then, as if he had fully explained things, he turned around and waited for the commercial, a commercial in which a balding and mustachioed store clerk was trying in vain to stop three women from molesting toilet paper, to end.

Officer Pete grabbed Chief Bosco's arm with his free hand and, his voice emerging with a croak, "Who the hell is that?"

Frank gave the obvious answer, "This is Gregory Glass, Miss Gabby's son."

Doc Tremblay then told Officer Pete about Gregory, much of which you know, and what happened after Gregory heard about his daddy's death. You see, Doc had Gregory transported as far as Baton Rogue to a psychiatric hospital there. He and Miss Gabby hoped someone could find a way to talk to the child, to explain what had happened, to get him to come terms with the grief that a son feels at learning of the death of his father. But no one could. Each time he came out of sedation he would thrash at his restraints, bellowing "107 days" over and over again. After a week like this, Doc Tremblay and the other physicians involved were convinced that Gregory was going to have to remain sedated for the foreseeable future, if not forever. They mentioned long term psychiatric care for the boy, and discussed a place in Jackson, since it wasn't so far away that she could not visit on a regular basis.

But Miss Gabby had other ideas. She called Officer Bosco and explained her plan. Bosco, if truth be known, was in love with Gabby, had been since high school where she treated him like a favorite little brother, and despite his own thought that Miss Gabby was as crazy as a bed bug, he spoke to his uncle the Mayor and they had built for her the house within a house in which Gregory would spend the rest of his life. Reliving his last happy day. And for the next forty years, Gregory Glass woke up to July 31, 1967. Every morning, his mother would, right after Gregory dressed himself in his favorite cowboy clothes, right after a breakfast of eggs, bacon and Tang, right after Gregory took his pills, hand him a pair of scissors and he would clip off the number 108, showing that his father would be home in less than four months.

And as time passed for the rest of the world, Miss Gabby would wake up every morning long before dawn and replace the paper time line that she had prepared for him to track the days until his father came home. Then she would, as close as humanly possible, let him live the day before they learned of Lt. Glass' death. And every night after she had given him his pills, read him Esphyr Slobodkin's book, "Caps for Sale" (one of Captain Kangaroo's favorite books), tucked him in and put him to sleep, Miss Gabby would take stock of what needed to be mended, what needed to be replaced, what DVDs needed to be reset for the following morning. Then she would lock up the little house from the inside and go to sleep in her bedroom, a bedroom which, like Gregory's, looked, as close as humanly possible, just the same as it did on July 31, 1967.

As Doc Tremblay told his story, Gregory had shifted his chair to watch the men and, more importantly, to listen, his face turning from doughy and white to splotchy and crimson as he did so. Apparently realizing that his world was about to have an unfortunate collision with reality, Gregory Glass screamed, "Bad man!" and pulled his gun from his holster. He pointed it at Doc Tremblay. He pulled the trigger. Pete's instinct took hold: he put three rounds into the center of Gregory's chest, killing him instantly. Gregory's pistol was a cap pistol, an original from the 1960s. In the 1960s, toy cap guns didn't have orange tips to indicate that they weren't the real thing.

Gregory's body slid to the floor, resembling now a dolphin's corpse washed up on a beach; there seemed to be very little human about it. I stuck my pipe in my mouth and ruminated a bit. I had long wondered what I would feel when my son died. As far as Gabby, since our vows had only been "until death do us part," I had felt nothing watching her die, other than a slight twinge of relief and the faintest whiff of guilt. Despite his being my only son, my blood, I felt nothing more than happiness at finally being released, being able to move on after more than forty years, rocking in a chair, chewing on the memory of a pipe, waiting. You see, a spirit can't leave the earth so long as his loved ones refuse to admit that he's gone. And Gabby, in her desire to keep Gregory from feeling pain, had trapped me here to the end of their days. Purgatory is a rocking chair. I glanced at the strip of paper on Gregory's wall, followed it down to the number 107. It had been a long tour of duty. And as yet another ambulance arrived, as Gregory was strapped on yet another gurney amidst the general hubbub of a police investigation, I departed.

# BUILDING A BETTER SPACESHIP

## Corey Pajka

Seven years. Seven long years spent amongst the hostiles on that barren planet had been enough. The time had come to take off.

Pressed against the corrugated floor of the starship Maytag, Captain Jamie Hobbes initiated a final launch procedure checklist.

Flaps fastened, engines primed, cardboard carburetors flowing freely, corners taped, staples removed, linoleum launch pad stabilized. There would be no mistake this time. Liftoff was inevitable.

Trial runs complete, the prototypes tested, torn down, rebuilt from scratch and tested again. Margin of error had been reduced to a non-zero possibility. Captain Hobbes had spent the last month in preparation for this moment, building a better cardboard spaceship. There would be nothing to stand in his way this time.

"Jamie, what are you doing in there?"

His mother yelled from the television room over the roar of the clanking wheel on the set. A live studio audience clapped in approval as the real estate agent from Des Moines correctly guessed "Pittsburgh Steelers Wheel" in the "Before and After" category.

"You haven't gotten into the spare boxes again, have you?" she bellowed back, her speech underscored by the rattle of ice in her vermouth. "We save those for moving."

"I'm okay, mom. I'm just getting ready for takeoff," the Captain replied with an air of obviousness. Even through the cloud of cigarette smoke that separated Captain Hobbes from his parents, his intents should have been clear.

"Godspeed to you, Captain Hobbes," Dad blurted, fading in and out of a Valium-induced sleep. He awoke long enough to yell for the housewife from Duluth to buy a vowel.

"Thanks, Dad. Thank you."

Captain Hobbes digressed from the distraction of the planet's hostiles and returned to the task at hand.

Atmospheric conditions were far from hospitable. Captain Hobbes' window of opportunity for a successful launch would be finite, and at best, minute.

Strong pressure in the lower atmosphere would make for a choppy ignition. Initial velocity would be crucial in building necessary inertia to break free of the especially strong gravitational pull of this barren alien world. The odds stood against the courageous Hobbes that day, but he was no stranger to adversity. Challenge was the old friend and confidante that urged him further and pressed him on to overcome. The trials of seven years had taught him that much.

No force on Earth or beyond would deny him this conquest, this ascent, this preordained escape to the heavens that beckoned him from above. All his life, Captain Hobbes had been an inmate of prison planet, Paramus, New Jersey. Captain Hobbes lived as one of them, laboring by their side. He had been assigned, as they all were, to the existence of the cube.

Each day he rode their yellow aluminum shuttle to the holding cell of brick and steel, enduring the conformity trials. Captain Hobbes was swept along the current of this river of deceit. He was made to learn and recite their hymns of institutional learning, and given marks of aptitude based on accurate repetition.

When his recitation was worthy of merit, he was given a reward. When it merited discipline, he was subjected to the trial of "time out."

The blue print of assimilation was laid out. He saw his own life progress before him in ascending levels of conformity. From elementary school, he would be subject to matriculation, and conferred with a paper of expertise in some arbitrary field of concentration. There he would elevate to the highest level of compliance, the stage known as "occupation."

Much like his parents, he was to look forward to a lifetime in a box such as those they had chosen. A cube reality of finite dimension, unadaptable to the whims of his fancy.

The planet was indeed box-shaped, a cubicle of adulthood proceeded by the wooden coffer of burial. It was a dreary box he inhabited. Seven years of desolation, and Captain Hobbes deigned that he would not allow himself to be confined to this menial, misshapen existence. An exit must exist.

Answers were slow to arrive. Each day demanded more of the Captain in this cubist continuance. Each period of absorption and bewilderment was rounded out by meals eaten in silence around the flickering light of the television. His parents, silent and blank-faced, brought him no voice of comfort or rationale. One night, out of the reticence, Jamie asked why he needed to attend this place called "school" or why they went to the place called "work." One baffled answer came forth.

"Because, Jamie, that's just the way things are."

Later that night, Captain Hobbes descended to the living room. At the coffee table, he leafed through an unexplored stack of yellow-bordered magazines by the footstool.

The pictures beheld it all, a realm of limitless unknown adventure past the confines of the box world. He attended photos of the man named Armstrong as he walked on the moon. Hobbes marveled at the woman named Ride in the space shuttle, and the boundless depths that lay beyond the limits of even his own vivid imagination.

Captain Hobbes' mind was made up. He could no longer live within the walls of the prison Planet Paramus, the Box World. The life of cubes and confinement would not be tolerated. He would blast off, up, up, and away from it all. On the day the new dishwasher was delivered to the house, he knew. Captain Hobbes had found his vessel.

The box was ideally shaped for a space traveler his size; brown and rectangular, and with just enough headroom to ensure comfort and mobility. The Captain set about making it worthy of deep space travel.

Initial trial runs did not go well. A false takeoff one day, and a near burnout the next threatened to derail his mission. Malignant weather throughout that week made the going even more difficult as building commenced, but Captain Hobbes would not be undone.

Each day, following his learning trials, reconstruction of the craft was his obsession. Crayolas in hand and Elmer's glue by his side, Captain Hobbes strove to concoct the space ship he saw in his dreams. He would not rest until the Starship Maytag saw her maiden voyage.

The Captain knew and heard nothing of television. Childish games and distractions became mere distractions. Trifles such as geography and mathematics were swept aside. Nothing stood between Hobbes and his great mission. The only box he knew and felt was that before him.

On the day of the great snowfall, two days into the New Year, conformity rituals were cancelled in the interest of creating a safer transit path. All else had been set aside in the aftermath of the great white blizzard.

The moment was now. He felt it in the very core of his being. The day of the launch had at last come.

That morning he left a goodbye note to his parents by the television, knowing they would find it there.

"Do you think we should worry about this?" Mom had asked Dad when she read it.

"It's just some game he's playing," Dad inspirited, "he'll be over it soon enough."

"I'm not sure, is this what they refer to as a warning sign?"

"Honey, we've all got the day off today. If Jamie has found something to keep himself occupied, then I'm over the moon about that."

Formalities behind him, Captain Hobbes completed a final diagnostic scan. All was in place. Countdown could commence at last.

"Mom, Dad," he cried from within the starship, "I'm taking off now."

"That's nice, Jamie," Mom answered.

"Watch out for Uranus, son," Dad chimed in.

"Dear!"

Within the cardboard cubicle, Hobbes endured the immediate shock of ignition. The jolt shook him with unanticipated violence. Lesser men would have yielded under the force, broken and begging for mercy, but Captain Hobbes would not relent.

He had fought too hard and struggled too long to surrender now, seven years was too long a prison sentence to resume his toil. Hobbes ground his teeth, and pulled the nearest lever, summoning more fiery propulsion.

"Hey, do you feel something shaking?" Mom asked.

"Yeah," Dad snorted, fully awake, "what is that?"

The foundation of the house quaked as the engine heightened the inferno.

Clocks, portraits, and a cacophony of wall hangings dislodged and shattered on the tile floor, flotsam from the shipwreck. Flame enveloped the kitchen and spread out to the television room.

Mom and Dad bounded out the back door, shouting over the hellfire that engulfed the house.

"STOP, JAMIE! TURN IT OFF!!"

Their shouts were unheard.

"TEN."

From within his tiny cockpit...

"NINE."

Jaime saw only the motion of hands...

"EIGHT."

The silent screaming of mouths...

"SEVEN."

The gnashing of yellowed teeth...

"SIX."
Hacking coughs...
"FIVE."
Receding hairlines...
"FOUR."
Bloated stomachs...
"THREE."
Wasted dreams...
"TWO."
Squandered potential...
"ONE."
Broken hearts...
"LIFTOFF."
...and acceptance of the box life.

The Maytag rose forth from its linoleum launch pad. Volcanic momentum cast away the bindings of the house like a discarded shell.

The box penetrated the ceiling, burst through the attic, and out the roof leaving a vapor trail of shingles and wood in its wake.

Clouds whipped past the cockpit window like wisps of smoke. His parents and the gathering crowd of panicked neighbors dissolved into dots of terrain along the landscape that grew smaller by the second. Planet Paramus and its cube-shaped trappings were little more than features on the shrinking globe below.

Blue dissolved to black. The moon came into view as the Maytag darted betwixt the infinite pinpoints of light in the ocean of dark, limitless space.

The red hue of Mars would follow, then the rocky asteroid belt. Then would come Jupiter, and then beyond the infinite reaches of the Milky Way into unknown space.

Captain Jamie Hobbes was never heard from again.

# HEADLESS IN NEW YORK

## Glenn Gray

Fred thought it was funny the first time his head fell off. He carried it around under his arm for a while like a basketball and chuckled and all he could think of was the guy from that movie, The Reanimator.

He didn't think that could happen in real life but here he was in his living room, holding his head in his hands overhead, arms outstretched, looking in the complete opposite direction his body faced. He could see his back and ass in the mirror.

He still couldn't figure out how he was able to breathe but the opening to his trachea was patent at the top of his neck and by the swishy sounds he knew air was getting sucked into his lungs somehow. And he guessed his brain was getting oxygen by osmosis or diffusion or something.

The fact that he could see didn't surprise him since the eyeballs connected directly to the brain via the optic nerves and chiasm. Thank God for his anatomy and physiology classes.
The arteries and veins seemed to just clamp up too. Seal off like a zip-lock bag.

Wow.

He could get things back to normal if he pushed his head hard on the top of his neck and sort of gave it a back and forth motion. It seemed to stay in place but he didn't want to take any chances by doing anything that involved any jerky motions. He found he could pop it back off too with the same kind of motion, but with a little force.

He remembered that first night. He had gotten home from work and had his usual snack of crackers and cheese and then he went down for a nap.

When he woke, there was his head - down by his feet looking up between his legs. What a sight he had. At first he thought someone else was in the bed with him and that really freaked him out but when he tried to move, the body above him obeyed. He thought about something and it just happened.

And that part he just couldn't figure out - even still. There was no neural connection between his brain and his body, yet his brain, from a distance, could control the body like a remote-control car.

He had watched his body lose its cool as he freaked out. He watched his frantic hands rub their way around his body, grasp at the empty space above his neck, run around in circles a bit and then cautiously step over to the head, cup it in the palms of its hands as if holding a sacred gauntlet, slowly lift and clumsily put it back on his neck.

And then he laughed.

\* \* \* \*

The next day Fred got up for work and his head was right where it was supposed to be. He thought maybe he had been dreaming but when he stood in front of the bathroom mirror with his palms against the sides of his head and he gave a combination twist and push there it was again, his head popped right off.

He brushed his teeth by suspending his head by a clenched fist of hair real close to the mirror and brushed with the left. He dangled his head real close to the mirror to get a good look and was able to angle just right to get the shadows away. Something he couldn't do before. So there was an advantage.

He wondered what other advantages there were to this situation.

Just for kicks he swung his head around by the hair and was able to get a unique view of his ass – a perspective he had never seen before. He didn't know if this was an advantage or not.

He laughed again.

\* \* \* \*

His early morning walk to the subway station on 86th and Lex was uneventful. His head was back in place and he looked like everyone else.

He wore a baby-blue collar shirt with a red spotted tie, snug around his neck. He was in the first car so that he could see the tracks barreling toward the train at the front window. Since it was Saturday, there was only one other person in the car, mid-way through, face buried in the New York Post.

At 77th Street a homeless person stumbled on. Tattered clothes and fisting a load of dirty, ripped shopping bags full of nothing. He sat down and started mumbling.

Fred decided to sit too, though a good distance away from the smelly street guy. He massaged his neck and could see his own reflection in the window across the car. He smiled.

He looked normal.

The train rocked and stuttered around a curve. There was loud screeching of metal wheels on metal track. The lights flickered.

There was an abrupt halt and start and the motion was something like whiplash and before he knew it his head was rolling down the center aisle.

Fred could see the posters and advertisements along the wall, spiraling around, alternating with the cans and bottles and crumpled paper under the seats.

His head thudded against the front door and then started back down the aisle toward his body and he could intermittently see his headless form sitting there and he told it to lean down and reach and it did and he scooped up his head like a shortstop in the infield.

He quickly popped it back on; having to loosen the tie quickly with one hand first but there it was, back in place. He pushed down hard on the top of his head and then shot a look over at the homeless guy, who had a weird grin on his face.

Fred said, "Morning."

The guy cackled and smacked his lips.

The other guy reading the paper hadn't moved.

Fred laughed.

* * * *

Fred couldn't concentrate at work. He hated doing Saturdays too. He sat in his cubicle, pretending to be on the phone, pretending to write on a blank pad.

He decided to do an internet search. See if there were any other cases like his. He searched things like, "Head falling off," and all he got were a bunch of jokes and songs and some prank videos.

Nothing serious. He then stumbled onto one of those medical sites with its own search. He tried more medical type terms like "cranial detachment" and "headless" but found nothing at all similar to his situation. Seemed there were no other cases of someone's head falling off at the shoulders and living to tell about it.

He figured it was time to see a doctor.

* * * *

"So, Fred," the doctor said. "Tell me exactly what you're feeling one more time."

Fred was sitting on an exam table, in a gown. The doctor sat on a stool directly in front of him.

"Well," Fred said. "The other morning I woke up and my head was off. You know, detached from my body."

"You mean it felt like it was detached, no?"

"No. I mean it was really off. I picked it up and carried it around."

"Well, didn't it hurt?"

"Not at all."

"And you found you could still breathe? And think and see?"

"That's the crazy thing. I just can't figure that out. I mean, I even move my body from across the room. I was quite frightened at first, but now I think it's kind of cool. Even funny."

"No bleeding?"

"Not a drop."

"Well, Fred. I don't know what to say. I must admit, I've never come across this. You would certainly be worthy of writing up. A definite medical case report."

I did a web search myself. Found nothing like my case."

"Well, I suppose I should have a look, no?"

"Should I pull it off now?"

The Doctor stood. "No no no. Not yet." The doctor pulled a stethoscope from the pocket of his white coat. "Let me examine you first."

* * * *

Fred sauntered down Third Avenue near 34th Street looking down at the prescription in his hand. The doctor had ordered an MRI of his brain and cervical spine. Just to check, he had said.

So Fred called the Radiology Center the doctor recommended near NYU and the receptionist had told Fred, sure come on over now. We're not that busy today and we just had a cancellation.

So off he went.

Fred couldn't believe that the doctor didn't want him to pull off his head right then and there. The doctor told him that he would be worried, if his head was off and something went wrong. He had no experience with that sort of thing and wouldn't want to be caught unprepared."

That kind of made sense, Fred thought after a while.

* * * *

"Fred Tibbles?"

"That's me."

"I'm Steve, the MR tech. I'll be doing your scan. I just need to take some history."

"Okay."

"Do you have any metallic devices in your body? Valves, clips, pacemakers, wires, anything of that sort?"

"Nope."

Any past surgeries?"

"Nope."

"Wallet, keys, credit cards. All metallic objects in the locker?"

"Yup."

"Why did your doctor send you? What's the reason for the scan?"

Fred cleared his throat. "Well, my head comes off my body and I can reattach it."

Steve stared.

Fred couldn't read his face. There was a smirk blurred together with the slightest hint of anger.

Steve, the tech, didn't say anything.

Fred finally said, "I'm serious."

Steve said, "Just hop up on the table here."

* * * *

On Monday Fred got a call from the doctor's office. The message was to call right away and please come over to the office. The doctor wanted to see him.

Fred called and said he'd come by at lunch, around 12:30.

The receptionist said okay.

* * * *

"Well, Fred," the doctor said. "The Radiologist faxed over the report from your MRI today and then he followed up with a phone call."

"Yeah?"

"They don't always do that. I mean, he thought the findings warranted a special call."

"That's interesting."

"Yes, that's what the Radiologist said."

"So?"

"I looked at the study too. Just because I had to see for myself. See, there's a band of abnormal signal across your cervical spinal cord. At about the C4 to C5 level."

"Okay. English, Doc."

"Well the Radiologist felt that this was related to some kind of trauma. Almost as if the cord had been severed. Said he'd never seen it before."

"I see the case report coming for sure now, Doc." Fred smiled.

"And there was air in the disc space at that level. Really strange. And then he told me that there was this abnormal appearance to the soft tissues in a ring-like configuration at that level. All around the neck."

"Kind of makes sense, no Doc? I mean with what I been telling you and all?"

"Well it just can't be. I mean you must have had some kind of trauma. You must have had a concussion too. Have you been in a car accident or hit your head recently?"

"Not at all. Told you. Just woke up the other morning and there was my head. At the foot of the bed."

The doctor took a deep breath. "Very well," he said. His voice was crackly and he had a very stern, serious expression. His hairy eyebrows furrowed.

He stared at Fred.

"I can't believe I'm saying this. But, here it goes. Fred, please take off your head."

Fred grinned, satisfied. He sat up straight, inhaled deeply, let it out. He methodically placed his hands on the sides of his head, exaggerating his motions slightly like a magician. His fingers fanned so that the thumbs were behind the ears and his pinky fingers crossed his eyebrows.

Fred winked at the doctor. "Ready, Doc?"

The doctor nodded slowly.

Fred gave the old push and twist motion and there was a shucking sound.

The doctor slid from the stool to the floor.

Fred's head came off, and he stood pole-straight, holding it high in the air with both hands, the tooth-filled grin still on his face.

# ROB PLATH

## baudelaire's ghost is better than the sandman

i couldn't sleep
4 a.m.

i shut my eyes
cursing

that's when baudelaire's ghost
showed up

he had some poor shit's soul
under his one arm & in the other
a phantom cheese grater

he kept shaving soul motes
over my face

sprinkling flakes beneath
my weary lids

& as my eyes grew heavier
he began whispering
misanthropic slogans in my ear

"the body isn't a temple
it is a shithouse"

& so on & so forth...

i awoke at 11 a.m.
rewired like a motherfucker

# JOHN DORSEY

**walt whitman has diabetes**
**(for spider)**

he smiles at me
skin dead and dying
on the 4th floor
of a south toledo rehabilitation center

he crushes a ginkgo nut with his bicep
and says that if it smells like puke
that's just karma

he reminds me that we've met before
though not in these bodies
but during lenin's revolution

says he was a kite maker
for benjamin franklin

says he was a feminist
before it was cool

says he shouted accusations at mary shelley

says he was the monster & the torch

on a clear night stars gaze upon him
and wonder is new jersey really celestial?

says that's really too much to think about

says they will only call you a genius
right before they are about to murder you

says he was never himself
but that the whitman body

has just been his favorite

he says when he gets out of here
we will roast marshmallows
on the first willing crucifix

he says not to worry
in the meantime
children will still die of cancer
while old men chew
on the bones of prunes

# CONTRIBUTORS' BIOS

## Zachary Amendt

Zachary Amendt is the author of Casa de Serenidad, which was recognized as a 2007 "Notable Story" by storySouth and reissued in Dzanc Books' 2008 "Best of the Web" anthology. He is a former resident of Coachella, Calif.; currently he works as a grant writer for the San Francisco AIDS Foundation.

## Tom Badyna

Tom Badyna is from New Suffolk, New York.

## Katherine Conner

Katherine Conner's stories have appeared in the Press 53 anthology Surreal South, The Chattahoochee Review, issue 55 of The Portland Review, and in issue 56 of The Portland Review. She graduated with her Ph.D. in Creative Writing from Florida State University.

## Carl Michael Daniels

Carl Miller Daniels is 58 years old. He currently lives in ruggedly masculine Homerun, VA. Over the years, his poems have appeared in lots of nice places: Chiron Review; CommonLine E-Journal; FUCK!; My Favorite Bullet; Nerve Cowboy; Pearl; Thieves Jargon; Wormwood Review; Zen Baby; Zygote in my Coffee; and 5AM, to name a few. Daniels has had two chapbooks published in the past dozen years or so: Shy Boys at Home (published by Chiron Review Press), and Museum Quality Orgasm (published by Future Tense Books). The poet Antler wrote the following comment for Daniels' chapbook Shy Boys at Home, and Antler's comment appears on the cover of that chapbook: "Carl Miller Daniels' poems incarnate youthful gay sexuality with gentleness, passion and delight. Shy Boys at Home is a unique contribution to the renaissance of gay poetry in America at the beginning of the new Millennium." (Nice comment, huh?) On three separate occasions, Daniels has been nominated for a Pushcart Prize. He and his lover, Jon (aka "the sweetest man in the world"), have lived together for over 30 years.

## John Dorsey

John Dorsey currently resides in Toledo, OH. He is the author of *Harvey Keitel, Harvey Keitel, Harvey Keitel* with S.A. Griffin and Scott Wannberg, Butchershop Press/Rose of Sharon Press/Temple of Man, 2005, and *Moshing With The Cosmos* with Iris Berry, Magenta Press, 2005. He can be reached at *archerevans@yahoo.com*

## Michael Fedo

Michael Fedo's books include *The Lynchings in Duluth*, *The Man From Lake Wobegon*, and the novel *Indians in the Arborvitae*. His next book, *A Sawdust Heart: My Vaudeville Life in Medicine and Tent Shows* by Henry Wood as told to Michael Fedo will be published in 2111 by the University of Minnesota Press.

## Glenn Gray

Glenn Gray is a physician specializing in Radiology. He's got stories in the 1st Beat to a Pulp Anthology, the 3rd Thuglit Anthology and Zygote in my Coffee's 8th print edition. He has stories in OOTG 3, 5 and 6 and many places online. He lives in New York.

## John Grey

John Grey is a Australian born poet and US resident since the late seventies. He works as a financial systems analyst. He has been published in Slant, Briar Cliff Review, Albatross, Poetry East, Cape Rock and REAL.

## John Grochalski

John Grochalski's poems have appeared in Avenue, The Lilliput Review, The New Yinzer, The Blue Collar Review, The Deep Cleveland Junkmail Oracle, The ARTvoice, Modern Drunkard Magazine, The American Dissident, Words-Myth, My Favorite Bullet, The Main Street Rag, Thieves Jargon, Underground Voices, Why Vandalism, Eclectica, Zygote In My Coffee, Gloom Cupboard, the Kennesaw Review, Re)Verb, Octopus Beak Inc., Clockwise Cat, The Smoking Poet, Ink, Sweat, and Tears, and Cherry Bleeds. His fiction has appeared in the Pittsburgh Post-Gazette, Pequin, and will be forthcoming in the anthology Living Room Handjob. Grochalski's column The Lost Yinzer appears quarterly in The New Yinzer (www.newyinzer.com), and his book of poems *The Noose Doesn't Get Any Looser After You Punch Out* is out via Six Gallery Press. Grochalski currently lives in Brooklyn, New York, and is a librarian at the Brooklyn Public Library.

## Tim Hawkins

Tim Hawkins has lived and traveled widely throughout North America, Southeast Asia and Latin America where he has worked as a journalist, technical writer and teacher in international schools. He currently lives in his hometown of Grand Rapids, Michigan. His poems have appeared recently in Umbrella: A Journal of Poetry and Kindred Prose, The Shit Creek Review, The Literary Bohemian, BluePrintReview, Underground Voices, 13 Miles from Cleveland, and The Flea.

## Sean C. Hayden

Sean Hayden's short fiction has appeared or is forthcoming in: All Hallows, The Dirty Goat, The Dunesteef Audio Fiction Magazine, Fickle Muses.com, The Griffin, Haight Ashbury Literary Journal, M-Brane SF, Necrography, Portland Review, Tabard Inn, and Westview.

## S. Hemming

S. Hemming is an occasional contributor to Underground Voices

## Allison Kade

Allison Kade is a seasoned freelance writer and an editor at LearnVest, a prominent personal finance website for women. Her fiction has been published in the literary magazine *Underground Voices*; in addition to developing more short stories, she is currently writing a stageplay and a short film. Prior to joining LearnVest, she was the Columns Editor at GreenAndSave.com, an environmental news website. Her past ventures include teaching an online creative writing course for high school students and founding an international young adults' creative writing community that was featured as one of the 101 best websites for writers by *Writer's Digest*. Allison holds a B.A. from Columbia University and loves to travel. She is particularly drawn to writing that betrays a true love of language and the understanding that reality is what we make of it; her favorite books include *Kafka on the Shore, 100 Years of Solitude*, and *Midnight's Children*.

## Margaret Karmazin

Margaret Karmazin's publishing credits include over one hundred stories published in literary and national magazines, including *Rosebud, Chrysalis*

*Reader, North Atlantic Review, Potomac Review, Confrontation, Virginia Adversaria, Mobius, Chiron Review* and *Aim Magazine*. Her stories in *The MacGuffin, Eureka Literary Magazine, Licking River Review* and *Words of Wisdom* have been nominated for Pushcart awards and Piper's Ash, Ltd. has published a chapbook of her sci-fi, entitled "Cosmic Women." She is also an artist with work in *SageWoman, A Summer's Reading, The MacGuffin, We'Moon Calendar, Adirondack Review* and PA regional publications.

## Travis Mills
Travis Mills is a filmmaker, fiction writer, and photographer who draws on his experience living in. Africa and Europe for his work.

## Corey Pajka
Corey Pajka is an actor and writer living in Brooklyn, New York. He holds dual degrees in Theatre Arts and English with a concentration in writing from Wilkes University. He has worked extensively in regional and Off-Off Broadway theatre as well as several independent and student films. He is a founding member of the New York-based theatre company Genius Savant productions as a writer and performer in residence.

## Rob Plath
Rob Plath is a 40 year-old poet from New York. A former student of Allen Ginsberg, he has published hundreds of poems in the small presses. He has seven chapbooks out: *Ashtrays and Bulls* (Liquid Paper Press 2003), *An IV Bag Full of Bile* (Scintillating Publications 2007), *Whiskey and Clay* (Pudding House Publications 2008), *Squeezing Blood From The Alphabet* (Erbacce Press 2008), *Tapping Ashes in the Dark* (Lummox Press 2008), *There's A Little Hobo In My Heart Who Forever Gives The Finger To Humanity* (d/e/a/d/b/e/a/t press) and *Nicotine Scribblings From A Hammock In The Void* (Good Japan Press 2009 ). His first full-length book is *A Bellyful of Anarchy* (epic rites press 2009).

## Jim Ryals
Jim Ryals is a lawyer-turned-writer. His poems have been featured at xStream and TMPoetry. He is in the midst of writing a novel.

## Michael Shorb

Michael Shorb's work reflects his interest in combining the lyric and satirical modes while addressing real world issues and concerns. He writes frequently about environmental and political issues. His work has appeared in Nation, Michigan Quarterly Review, Commonweal, The Sun, Rattle, Underground Voices, Poetry Salzburg Review, Queen's Quarterly, and European Judaism.

## Barry Spacks

Barry Spacks is the first Poet Laureate of Santa Barbara, Californa. He has nine poetry collections (most extensive: SPACKS STREET: NEW & SELECTED POEMS, from Johns Hopkins, 1982, winner of The Commonwealth Club of California's Poetry Medal; most recent: REGARDING WOMEN, WordTech Communications, winner of the Cherry Grove Collections Prize, and THE HOPE OF THE AIR, Michigan State University Press, both 2004). He is a N.E.A librettist grantee; has performed many poetry readings; has poems in 18 anthologies and a multitude of journals, print and cyber; two novels, stories, essays, reviews. For poems and novels, he has been awarded the St. Botolph's Arts Award, Boston.He was a Literature professor at M.I.T. (1960-1981); persistently Visiting Professor, U.C. Santa Barbara (Distinguished Professor in Humanities & Fine Arts, 1991) and Senior Vajrayana (Tibetan Buddhism) student of H.E. Chagdud Tulku Rinpoche. He also has two CDs: *A Private Reading*, from WC Studios, containing 42 poems (plus chat) from 50 years of work and *Selected Poems from Regarding Women.*

## Justin Wade Thompson

Justin Wade Thompson was born in New Braunfels Texas and currently lives in a trailer park in East Austin. He has never pursued a higher education, career, or held a full-time job.

www.ingramcontent.com/pod-product-compliance
Lightning Source LLC
Chambersburg PA
CBHW020628250626
47154CB00004B/1713